This is a work of fiction. Names, characters, places, and incidents either are the product of the author's imagination or are used fictitiously. Any resemblance to actual events, locales, organizations, or persons, living or dead, is entirely coincidental and beyond the intent of either the author or the publisher.

Happy Medium: a Club Raven novel
By Julia Talbot
Copyright © 2017

Evil Plot Bunny LLC
PO Box 722
Loughman, FL 33858

Cover illustration by Erin Dameron-Hill
Published with permission

ISBN: 978-1-942831-38-9

Happy Medium
A Club Raven Novel
by Julia Talbot

Happy Medium

Dedication – To my wife BA Tortuga, and to Kiernan Kelly, who both understand the cast of thousands and participate eagerly.

Happy Medium: A Club Raven Novel

Chapter One

The low gaslight in the creaky old parlor cast the perfect glow on the round table, lending atmosphere to the cheap crimson cloth Max had draped over it. A candle or two would complete the look, but he wouldn't light them until immediately before the family assembled in the room.

He surveyed the seating. Seven chairs.

Max blinked, then frowned. He'd been told five family members and himself. Where had the extra chair come from and why?

He ducked back across the hall into the men's parlor, where he'd asked the family to allow him to be alone to prepare for the séance. Max took a deep breath, rubbing his fingertips over his watch chain, which hung across his waistcoat. Changing the plan was against the rules. The Marsten family should know that. He'd been incredibly clear. After another inhalation, he knelt beside the large carpet bag holding all his tricks and pulled out a piece of white cheesecloth and a small glass orb. Those would serve as his floating spirit. The glass orb would be far more mysterious than the rubber balls some of his contemporaries used. He needed these and a picture of the deceased.

Many men had tried to debunk the Mesmerizing Maximillian and failed. That was because, while he might not be able to talk to the dead, Max didn't have to resort to wires and dressed up actors for his tricks. He rubbed his fingers against his thumb, feeling his calluses slide together. Then he stopped, glaring at his hand. No tells. No nervous habits. Get this over with, get the other half of his payment, and move on.

Closing his eyes, he rubbed his hands on his pants, then nodded sharply. Time to set up. Max grabbed some tallow candles scented with a tiny bit of sage, the orb and cloth, and a few other tricks from his bag.

Thank God the parlor was still empty. The family waited in the dining room for his signal, sipping port or brandy in an effort to steel their nerves, no doubt. Contacting a dead relation always gave people pause, and for good reason. Inviting such things into your home, finding out information you didn't want to know, was always a risk. Even with a charlatan like him, there was a chance of summoning something real. When that happened, if it did, his only backup plan was to run.

He thought of what had happened in Philadelphia and shuddered.

Max couldn't think of that now. Candles, drunkards' matches, the orb hidden behind the biggest chair. He placed a few atmospheric touches about, then lowered the gas lamps in the chamber.

Time to go get the family. He needed to lead them in, sort them out so they sat where he needed them to.

He strode to the dining room and knocked on the door, which swung open easily. Clearly the portal was meant to allow servants easy access with trays. This had been a proud house once, beautiful. Now it was run down and sad.

"I'm ready, Mr. Marsten," Max murmured in a low, respectful tone.

"Thank you." The gentleman of the house rose, his moustache twitching with distaste. Clearly he was indulging his wife with this séance; the lady in question still wore deep mourning rather than the gray and lavender sported by the other family members, so even though the death had been some time ago, she was unwilling to let go.

A man Max hadn't met rose from the table with the daughter and two spinster aunts. Tall, broad through the shoulders, he had the carriage of a soldier, not a bit of slouch about him. He held his hat in his hand, and his hair, cut too short for fashion, shone bright gold under the gas lamps. His handsome face creased in a smile, lines crinkling up beside his blue eyes and his mouth.

"I hope you don't mind that Miss Marsten invited me to attend," the fellow said. "Andrew Meechum, at your service."

"Maximilian." He nodded curtly, noting that Mr. Meechum didn't specify which Miss Marsten had asked him along. Both spinster aunts and the daughter went by that designation, so the ruse was a clever one, since all three ladies wiggled and fluttered when Meechum said the name. "I wish I had been informed ahead, but no matter if you come with an open mind." Max gave a strained smile.

"I do." Meechum spread his hands, apparently trying to look harmless. He managed about as well as a fox in the henhouse. "I am entirely at your disposal."

"Mmm." Max turned on his heel and left the room, the ladies preceding the gents as they all trooped over to the parlor. He stopped to light matches, touching them to the candlewicks. One of the spinsters, he could remember neither name, lowered the gas lamps even more, and the atmosphere changed immediately. No longer shabby or cheap, the room, and Max's additions, glowed in the candlelight, taking on an otherworldly cast that completely suited his purposes.

They settled at the round table where he imagined the family playing cards, the wife on one side of him, but Meechum sitting on the other where Mr. Marsten should be.

Max stared at the man, taken aback. "Are you a family friend, then?"

"Oh, yes." Meechum smiled at the assembly at large, his expression bland as butter. "We're tight as a drum."

He pursed his lips, but since no one argued any different, Max had to accept the lie. What was this man about? Why was he here, invading what should be a private family moment?

"Good. The people sitting next to me should have known the deceased." Max glanced at Mrs. Marsten. "You understand."

The matron looked to her husband, eyes wide. "Patrick—"

"Now, Anne," Mr. Marsten intoned, frowning at her repressively. "Let Andrew sit right where he is. It's fine."

Yes. So Meechum was a stranger. Max gritted his teeth to keep from shouting. He could confound even the best debunker and he knew it. No need to worry, even if he wasn't really a medium. Best to carry on as planned.

"Well, then. If we could all join hands?" Max reached for Mrs. Marsten's hand, which felt frail, dry. Rather like a bird's claw. On the other side, Meechum took up his hand, holding firmly. Warm, callused, that touch sent a thrill up his arm, raising the hairs there. His nipples hardened, and he fought the urge to fling off the grip and run. When had a man had such an effect on him? Well, at least since he'd reached full adulthood.

Max breathed slowly, in and out, centering himself. He had to be able to concentrate to pull this off. In. Out. He could do this, even with a very attractive stranger about.

"If everyone would close their eyes, please, with the exception of Mrs. Marsten. Madame, this is the pocket watch you wish me to use, yes?" He indicated the pocket watch next to picture of the lady's son.

"Yes." She said it through stiff lips, fear and anticipation burning brightly in her eyes.

"Good. You may now close your eyes, too." He stared hard at Meechum, whose lips were twitching madly.

He kicked the fellow under the table, and Mrs. Marsten jumped at the sound. "What was that?" she asked, looking wildly about.

"Your pardon, Madame. I kicked something."

"Oh." She relaxed her eager forward posture, her grip on his hand looser. She closed her eyes once more.

"Now, I must ask everyone to respect the circle we have created. Once I begin to contact your loved one we mustn't break the hold of our hands or flee. To do so would invite unwanted attention from the spirits into this home. Do you all understand?"

A soft chorus of assent told him he was ready to begin. Max narrowed his focus, steadying his breath, letting it flow in and out. He needed to clear his mind, let energy build inside his chest.

He blew out a slow breath, then began. "Spirits of the otherworld, we reach out to you. We beseech you, show us the way. This family has lost their beloved son, their dearest brother. They seek his restless soul, striving to offer him a path back to communicate his desires."

He cracked open one eye to make sure no one was peeking yet. They all sat still as statues, their eyes screwed tightly closed. Perfect.

The hardest part was waiting. Max wanted to get the show going right away, but he knew no one would believe it if he did. People had to be eased into things. They required a slow buildup in order to really be in the moment when it happened.

Another long exhale, then Max intoned, "Son of the Marsten family. Frederick, can you hear us? Give us some sort of a sign."

Mrs. Marsten was holding her breath next to him, and he hated to disappoint her, but he must this time. And the next. She would be on the edge of complete despair when he produced a sign from her son.

When no signal came, Mrs. Marsten sobbed lightly, her grip on his hand almost painful. She had nails as sharp and brittle as claws.

"This family needs a sign, Frederick. They miss you. They were no more ready for you to cross over than you were."

He knew the pertinent facts from his warm reading of Mrs. Marsten. Frederick Marsten, or Freddie as his mother called him, had been a happy-go-lucky fifteen-year-old lad. An avid bird hunter, he had been shot in the head by a friend, a terrible accident that had caused the friend to shoot himself nearly a month later, ending his own life as well.

They had buried their son, and by all accounts Mrs. Marsten had sunk deep into her own world, very much like Mrs. Lincoln had before the whole nation. Such a terrible thing to lose a child. A similar situation had cost Max a brother and his mother once upon a time.

Was what he did so bad, giving this lady hope? Hope could be a terrible emotion, but it had to be better than sinking into deep misery and ignoring your whole life.

The silence stretched out, and the man next to him made a muffled sound, almost a chuckle.

Max dug his thumbnail into Meechum's hand, a warning to shut his damned trap. He was at a critical moment in the process.

A grunt burst out of Meechum, and Mrs. Marsten started. "What? What is it?"

"Perhaps someone is trying to speak to us," Max drawled out. "We must be patient."

There was a shuffling of feet, then everyone settled again, faces creased in concentration. They were nearly there.

"Freddie. Your mother misses you so badly. Please give us some sort of sign that you miss her as well."

Now was the time for the first signal. The knocking. Max knew the value of following a relatively standard script for his séances. Staying with what was familiar to amateur spiritualists helped credibility.

He drew on the energy of the actual people around him, grabbing a tiny bit of their life to create the sound of a knock on the door behind them.

Mrs. Marsten made to rise, but he held her down. "Do not break the circle!" Max shouted. "He is among us."

"Oh, for God's sake." That was Mr. Marsten, though he sounded more worried than impatient. Maybe he thought Mrs.

Marsten would be overset.

"Yes. Yes, knock again if you wish to join us, Freddie." Max made his tone deep and dramatic.

Three more knocks sounded, guided by his talent. The tiny block of wood banging the door right now would never be found. He would fling it out an open window before they moved on to the floating globe trick.

The candles sputtered with a tiny breeze, an illusion he had just mastered. The effort made sweat pop out on his head, but the effect was perfect since most of the assembled company had forgotten their eyes were meant to be closed.

Both maiden aunts murmured, and the hand holding his on Meechum's side tightened around his fingers. Someone was a bit surprised. Bully for him.

He let the silence stretch for dramatic effect. Too much stimulation too soon overwhelmed the audience, made the action which followed more difficult to accept.

Then Max pushed out with his mind, intent on poking Mrs. Marsten on the shoulder.

"Oh!" She half-rose, but he pulled her back down, as did her husband. "Something touched me!"

Meechum leaned, peering, and Max bit back a smile. Family friend his arse. This man was a debunker, no doubt brought in by the husband, who thought all this was just so much horseshit. Someone intended to discredit him. Too bad there were no strings or extra actors to be found.

The orb would come next.

Max murmured some nonsense words, hoping they sounded different enough to come from a deeper realm than theirs. He threw his head back and opened his mouth wider, enunciating each sound with a bit of lip manipulation. He wished he could glow with ethereal light, but he hadn't figured out how to.

"The spirit pours through him!" one of the spinster aunts said. Really, he couldn't have paid them to do a better job for him. The timing was impeccable.

The orb now. This part took all his concentration, the weight of the orb and the cloth not challenging to lift, but to control. He had to make sure it didn't flail about the room, rather gliding smoothly. After several moments of concentration on his part, it rose from its place behind the credenza, dangling in the air. The cloth floated around the orb in a ghostly way, which pleased him immensely. He watched it out of the corner of his eye, trying for oblivious.

When no one else noticed it, however, he let the orb dip down over the table, doing a wee jig. Well, that was the tune in his head, any road. The orb might make it more a sea chanty, since it was so hard to control.

Now the assembled company gasped and jumped, the table moving when Mr. Marsten stood, still holding his wife and daughter's hands. "What is this madness!"

"Freddy! Freddy is that you?" Mrs. Marsten's tearful plea rang out, and it was almost enough to make Max feel bad. Only almost. He was giving her hope to keep her going, now wasn't he? If someone had done that for his mother, maybe things would have gone differently.

The orb dipped toward Mrs. Marsten as if nodding to her.

She shrieked loud enough his ears rang. "Oh, my Freddie. Oh, my boy. Thank you. Momma loves you. Why did you go?"

The daughter sobbed quietly, and the spinsters whispered to each other. Meechum stared at the globe for long moments, then turned a most disconcerting, knowing gaze upon Max. At least there were no wires to give him away here.

The orb was getting heavy, taxing his powers to hold it aloft. His ability was best used for short, sharp bursts of motion, not prolonged feats.

Max needed one more fantastical vision for the momma, so he squinted hard at the orb, building energy until it began to glow. Then he pushed hard with his mind, moving it up toward the rafters.

"Freddie, no! Don't leave me." As he had known she would,

Mrs. Marsten climbed to her feet, reaching for the orb.

It shattered then, exploding like a bomb, tiny glass shrapnel raining down on the table. He tried hard to shield Mrs. Martsen's face from the debris, not wanting her injured.

Meechum leapt to his feet to shield Mrs. Marsten from the glass as well, his arms over her head. The candles blew out, leaving them in a sullen gray room.

"Turn on the lights!" Mr. Marsten shouted, and one of the spinsters ran to raise the level of the gaslights. In the brighter light, poor Mrs. Marsten looked pale, her hands shaking. Her husband, on the other hand, was florid, his hands clenched into fists. "I swear, young man, if you faked this—"

He put on an affronted expression, drawing himself up with disdain. "I did not! Please, look for any wires, for anything that explains what just happened."

"I say—"

"Mr. Marsten, may I suggest you attend your wife?" Meechum nodded at Mrs. Marsten, who had slumped with her upper body on the table, sobbing.

Another glare at Max and Mr. Marsten took his wife away, lifting her and leading her out of the parlor.

"That was magnificent." One of the spinsters grabbed his arm, her hand a claw like her sister's. "Thank you, Great Maximilian."

"I'm so sorry if Mrs. Marsten is overset. These things are unpredictable." Max patted her hand, his nose twitching as he tried not to sneeze. She wore far too much rosewater.

"Of course." The daughter, who seemed a pragmatic type for one so young, rose and waved for him to follow. "Let me get your payment, sir."

"Thank you." He stood there, waiting, and everyone left the room save for Mr. Meechum, who Max stared at intently. "A family friend, did you say?"

"I am definitely on their side," Meechum returned. "That was quite a performance."

He didn't bat an eye. Staying cool with this type of doubter was the only option. "Did I cheat, then? Did I use wires or doubles?" Max knew the answer, knew this Meechum would never find proof that he was dishonest in any way.

"No. No mirrors, either, from what I can tell." Those arresting blue eyes, more like cobalt glass than the sky, bored into him. "There are other ways to cheat."

His heart leapt into his throat. "Are there? Well, you tell me what I did, and I'll prove you wrong." No one could know how he did what he did. He'd never met anyone else who could move things with their minds.

"I have to say, you're remarkable. I know that there was no spirit here, but the illusions were flawless."

Ah, clever man. If Max was an amateur, he might fall for the praise. Instead he sniffed in a haughty way, then took the payment Miss Marsten offered and turned away. "I'll just collect my bag and be on my way, miss."

"Thank you for everything, sir." She smiled, then turned to Mr. Meechum. "Father wishes to see you."

"Naturally." Meechum inclined his head to Max. "I hope we meet again, Maximilian."

"I'm sure." That was the best he could do. Max certainly didn't want to meet this man again.

He gathered his belongings, then pocketed his money and moved along. No lingering.

There was always someone else for whom to perform.

Chapter Two

I think he's doing it all with his mind," Andrew said. He swirled the brandy in his glass, watching the caramel colored liquor coat the sides of the vessel. He sat in the luxurious member lounge at his club, Club Raven. His dearest friend, Lionel James, sat directly across from him, coat flung over the back of the chair, one booted foot crossed over the opposite leg.

"Really? How entertaining."

"Mmm." He glanced at Lionel, who watched him carefully. Lionel was a powerful empath who rarely reacted to anything with more than light amusement, at least visibly. Undoubtedly he could feel how… conflicted Andrew was about this particular medium. "He certainly puts on a good show. He has another séance tomorrow, which I have arranged to attend."

"I see."

"Will you stop it?" Andrew set his brandy aside. "I have never been so anxious to see someone again and so reluctant to utterly debunk him."

"So you find him attractive." Lionel's dark eyebrows winged up.

That was the second best thing about Club Raven, wasn't it? That he was among men who enjoyed other men without censure. The best thing, of course, was that Andrew could be his whole self without hiding his talents. Exposing those abilities to the general public made for panic.

"I do." Andrew might as well admit it. "It's odd. He calls to me somehow. He's very alone, and I think he's scared. I have no idea what he's frightened of, because he's good at what he does, if untutored."

"So invite him to the club for supper." Lionel gave him an arch look. "If he sees that he's not the only one with such talents, perhaps he'll stop playing at confidence swindles and do something with his talent that matters."

"I wish I could believe that." Andrew couldn't understand what it was about the great Maximilian that intrigued him so. The young man was relatively unremarkable, with his dark brown hair and gray eyes, and while his talents were clearly considerable, he seemed only marginally aware of what they could do. Nevertheless, Andrew found himself utterly ensnared by the directness of that gray gaze, and the defiance he could detect.

"You need to stop agonizing and act. If not to bring him here than take him to a rented room and have your way with him."

"Lionel!"

"Well, wouldn't that be the best way to get him out of your system?"

"Stop." Now Andrew grabbed up his brandy glass again and drained it. "Really, you would think you felt as if you had a right to meddle in my private life."

"I did once upon a time." Lionel actually grinned at him now, a real expression of emotion. "I miss those days on occasion. Not enough to go back, naturally."

"Naturally. You're being quite the ass today."

"Am I?" Lionel snorted. "According to you, I generally do act that way. Shall we agree to disagree and play some billiards?"

"Sounds lovely." Andrew rose, tugging down his waistcoat. Something uncomplicated and not a bit argumentative. He and Lionel knew all of one another's cheats, so billiards was utterly safe.

After Lionel silently racked the balls and broke, it occurred to Andrew that Lionel might be suffering his own distress.

"Are you well?" he asked, staring intently at his friend.

"My father is rather ill," Lionel said, quite offhandedly.

"I am sorry." He knew Lionel and his father did not get on, but no one wanted to see a loved one falter.

"So am I. If the old bastard dies I will be forced to work for a living when I take over his concerns."

"Lionel!" He wasn't shocked, but propriety demanded he pretend.

"You know I have no interest in shipping."

"Hire a manager."

"I intend to, but one must check the figures every so often. Managers steal."

"Such a cynic you are. Have you no faith in human nature?" Andrew knew well that Lionel was too familiar with the race of man to be hopeful in outlook.

Lionel sank the three and four in quick succession. "None at all."

"Poor Lionel."

"We aren't discussing me, Andrew. We are talking about you and the false medium. What are you going to do?"

Andrew grinned wryly. "Why, crash his next séance, of course. From there, I shall be forced to play it by ear."

"Yes, well, just be certain you aren't playing in the wrong key, my dear. Such discord is never good for the soul." Lionel batted those sharp green eyes at him, the color like shards of emeralds.

"I will bear it in mind." He jostled Lionel's elbow, earning a laugh and a chance at a shot before Lionel ran the table.

Honestly, Andrew didn't care if he caused discord or not. What he really wanted was to see his young man again.

Chapter Three

When Max saw the man was there again he almost cancelled the séance. His palms began to sweat, and he blew out a frustrated breath.

The Meechum fellow could hardly be a family friend to this clan, as well. How was he doing it? How was he earning an invitation to Max's every performance?

This particular event was too important to cancel. The family, unlike the Marstens of his last séance, were rich as Croesus. They had lost three children to smallpox and typhus and one to war, and the matron of the house was adamant in her wish to contact all of them over the next several months. This could be a very lucrative situation for him if this Meechum man would simply leave him be and let him do his job.

He squared his shoulders before ducking under the curtain he'd erected at the back of the drawing room, and made his way across the room to stand next to Mr. Calloway and clear his throat. "Pardon me, sir."

"Are we ready to begin?" Calloway was florid and round, where his wife was thin as a rail. Gaunt.

"Not quite yet. May I have a word?" Max inclined his head to the other side of the room.

"Certainly." The man moved away from the friends and family who were milling about drinking brandy. "Is something amiss? Do you require a servant's help?"

"Your hospitality has been impeccable, sir. I wanted to inquire about Mr. Meechum. Why is he here?"

The man's bushy eyebrows winged up. "Andrew? He's a

friend of my younger brother. They frequent the same club, I understand. Do you know him?"

"No." He sighed. "I met him at another séance some days ago."

"Ah. Apparently he's an enthusiast." Calloway clapped him on the back. "Put on a good show for my dear wife, will you? She's gone 'round the bend, and this will give her something to live for."

"Yes sir." He hardly had to work at this one. Mr. Calloway was no believer, and his family had a stoic acceptance that the matriarch was quite mad. The dynamic made his job so much easier.

Now, what to do about Meechum, who was very much like a burr under his skin that he couldn't get rid of.

For the time being, Max decided to ignore the man. He would vent his spleen after he completed this particular farce and make sure Meechum never bothered him again.

He methodically checked all of his placements, all of the accoutrement to make certain Meechum had not tried to sabotage him by moving props or changing his safe areas by shifting furniture about.

Everything appeared to be normal as far as Max's world was concerned. Good. That was a fine thing. He tried to still the fluttering of his nerves, his breath shallow until he forced himself to breathe deeply. He had to do this. Calloway was willing to pay him two hundred and fifty dollars per séance. That would rent his boarding house room until his death in his ninetieth year, for God's sake, as well as all his meals.

He rolled his shoulders to release the tension there, then began closing curtains around the room. Time to start.

"Would you like me to gather the family?"

Max jumped, whirling to face Meechum. "Why are you here?"

"I'm here to watch your performance, of course. We both know you're not channeling spirits, but in this case, I don't feel as if you're defrauding anyone, since Mr. Calloway knows you're not for real."

"How very generous of you." His lips twisted. "Stay out of my way and let me do my job."

"I would never interfere once you begin. Breaking your concentration could be dangerous. Your control over your gift is tenuous enough."

Max's scalp prickled at the closeness of that dart. "What the hell do you know about me? Just leave me be!"

A low chuckle followed him when he turned on his heel and walked away. The sound slid down his spine, making him tingle, irritating him to no end. His reaction to this Meechum man was complicated, to say the least. Max preferred his life to be simple. Cut and dried.

"Ladies and gentlemen," he said to the guests assembled at the other end of the room. "We're ready to begin."

The shuffle began, all of them talking, the ladies tittering nervously. So familiar, and Max settled into his routine, steadfastly ignoring Meechum, who once again sat on his one side, holding his hand.

His palm felt sweaty, but with the older Calloway missus on his other side Max required calm and focus. He began, droning on about the same damned fake spiritual shit, sweat beading along his collar as well.

Mrs. Calloway gasped and clutched at his hand during all the right moments, but the whole thing felt lackluster. Maybe he needed to get a crystal ball or a planchette. The impact of those items on suggestive minds such as Mrs. Calloway's was strong. Time-tested. He could do far more than just the floating orb.

When it came time for the flickering candles, he overdid it, blowing them all out. Damn it all.

"Shall I call—"

"No! The spirit requires darkness to contact us!" No matter what he had to make it look as if every action was part of the plan.

"Oh! No lighting them!" The poor mothers were predictable. Max tried to understand, because no one should have to bury their children. God knew enough of them had to due to the damned war. So many people lost. So many.

Meechum squeezed his hand hard, and he realized the orb had dipped to rest on the table. He couldn't check his candle mark to tell how much time had passed. Time to shatter the orb and get this mess over with. Hopefully they would ask him back and he'd do a far better job next time.

The orb didn't explode. Max scowled at it. Then he pushed out with his thoughts, demanding it break. It bobbed in the air, defying him.

He sent a frantic glance at Meechum, who stared at the orb like the others. When Meechum looked at him finally, the man frowned.

"What the devil is going on?" Mr. Calloway rumbled.

"The spirit is having trouble piercing the veil," Max intoned. "Everyone close your eyes and call out to… it."

That gave him precious seconds to figure out what the hell was going on. Meechum nodded at the orb, his message obvious. What the hell?

What the hell indeed. How was he to do his job when his equipment failed him?

The orb zoomed all the way to the ceiling, then crashed back to the table, smashing into bits. Well, then. That was that.

A cry rose from Mrs. Calloway. "Charlotte! Look, husband. It's Charlotte's cameo there on the table."

Max started. What in the name of God? He stared hard at Mr. Calloway, who gave him a look of approval. Admiration, even.

"Looks as though she's saying hello, dear," Calloway boomed. "Well done, Maximilian. Well done."

"Thank you, sir." He kept his voice low, trying to work at being spent and shaky. The truth was, he had no idea what had just happened, so the sweat and the tremors in his hands were quite real.

"Allow me to help you back to your changing area, Maximilian," Meechum said. "That looks as if it took a great deal out of you."

He nodded, half rising before falling back into his seat to keep the illusion.

Mrs. Calloway sniffled and blew her nose into her hankie. "I'll ring for tea for him."

Meechum smiled at her before putting a hand under Max's elbow. "That would be a kindness, thank you. Come along, Max."

He went, because he wasn't certain his legs would hold him if he tried to walk on his own. Once they were out of earshot of the others, Max glared at Meechum. "Did you plan that with the old man?"

"Hell no, my boy. I was holding hands with you and with the widowed sister of the lady of the house. She dug in hard." Meechum showed him the half-moon marks of the lady's nails on the back of his hand.

"Well, shit." Max would regret the coarse language if anyone else overheard, but it seemed appropriate. "Do you think Mr. Calloway…"

"No, lad. He's not that clever." Meechum's expression held sympathy, and he wanted to smack the fellow.

"Damn." Max wiped his sweaty hands on his pants. "Do you think— I'm meant to do more work here? I've never had a real spirit."

"There may be other explanations." Meechum glanced over his shoulder as if to make sure no one was listening. "We can talk, but not here. Let me buy you a meal."

Max's eyes widened and he took a step backward. "No! Absolutely not."

"Why not? I can help you, lad." Meechum reached out, looking like he would enforce the words with a touch.

Max ducked. He couldn't bear for people to touch him. What if he lost control and defended himself with his mind and hurt someone?

"I won't hurt you, Max," Meechum soothed. "I vow it."

"I'm not worried about that." He stepped back another pace. "Please, just don't."

"Very well." Meechum held up both hands. "A meal. I shall buy. In a public place."

"I'm not hungry." His belly chose that moment to betray him, rumbling loudly.

"Yes, you are. There's a little establishment owned by a German family not far away. Boarding house food, but no need for us to dress formally. Come on."

He hesitated. This man already seemed to know his secrets. What could it hurt to have a free meal and find out what the hell Meechum wanted with him?

"Very well. Let me pack my things." He couldn't afford to get careless and leave his bag of tricks sitting about.

"Excellent." Meechum beamed for him, blue eyes crinkling at the corners in a most attractive way. "I'll meet you on the front porch."

Max nodded shortly and hurried to pack his valise. If there was a real spirit lurking in the Calloway house, he wanted no part of it.

Andrew waited, half expecting Max to leave him high and dry. The lad was the kind to bolt, after all. When Max appeared, valise in hand, Andrew had to admit he was impressed.

"There you are. It's a fine day out here. You hardly realize how gloomy these houses are."

"Perpetual mourning," Max murmured. "No joy is allowed when the lady of the house is so inclined."

"Perceptive. I suppose that's why you're so good at what you do."

"What is it you think I do?" Max asked, chin very firm, gray eyes serious.

"I think you put on a very good show for families who are desperate. I think you have the ability to move things with your mind, but you lose the finer details sometimes."

Max stopped dead, mouth falling open. Andrew took Max's elbow and guided him off the walkway, saving him from a grumpy older gent's cane.

Cheeks pale, Max tried to pull free. "No. I need to—"

"You need to eat." He tugged Max back into motion. "I'm not trying to harm you in any way, Max. I have a similar gift."

"So it was you with the orb!"

"No. I cannot move things with my thoughts. My mental talent is different," Andrew shrugged when Max glared. "Why would I deny it if I had done it? I've exposed both our secrets."

Max sighed. He put his feet down hard when he began walking once more. "I don't like the idea of a real spirit in there. In fact, it scares me."

"Neither do I, come to that." Andrew indicated a turn down a side street. The scent of schnitzel filled the air, and Andrew hummed happily.

"Oh, that smells good."

"I'm glad. I wouldn't steer you wrong." This place was small but mighty.

"How long have you lived here in the city?" Max asked when they ducked into Schmidt's.

"I came here just after the war."

"Did you fight?"

Andrew closed off memories that tried to swim to the surface. "For a year. Find a seat."

They settled at a long trestle table, sitting across from one another. Max stared at him intently for a moment, then nodded. "Sorry if I'm too nosy."

"It was a trying time for all of us," Andrew said by rote, brushing it off as he did all mentions of the fighting. "You should try the wiener schnitzel."

"As long as they have cabbage or stewed apples, I'll be a happy man."

"Herr Meechum. Good to see you." Frau Schmidt came to give him a glass of cool milk. "What would you like, son?"

"Coffee if you have it, ma'am."

"Ja." She bustled off again, humming some old country song. Andrew did adore her.

"This is a nice place. Clean."

"Precisely why I frequent it." Andrew did love the hidden gems of the city, the places where immigrants served native dishes with pride.

"A man like you surely has a club to go to."

"I do, in fact." That showed him something of Max's social status, didn't it? "I usually go there when I need an evening meal and companionship. I already have you here, and I feared the club might intimidate you."

"You mean I am not dressed for it."

Andrew inclined his head. "Neither am I, at least for the dining room. Perhaps next time." He intended for there to be a next time, for certain. Andrew had no idea why, but he was going to pursue the Mesmerizing Maximilian.

"Sure." Max scoffed, then hummed when Frau Schmidt brought coffee. "Thank you, ma'am."

"Mmm. You want schnitzel? Two with cabbage and apples? I heard."

"And bread, please, Hilda," Andrew added.

"Yes, sir." She left them again.

Andrew glanced back at Max. "Now, where were we? Ah, yes. I doubt Mr. Calloway or the sister did anything with the cameo. Did Mrs. Calloway ever release your hand?"

"No." Max chewed his lower lip. "No, I have the wounds to prove it." Max held out his hand, and sure enough, the imprint of Mrs. Calloway's nails was clear.

"Damn. Well, then, either someone else in the room has a talent similar to yours, which I highly doubt, or there was really a spirit present." Andrew frowned, worrying that over in his head.

Max tilted his head. "Why do you doubt it was a— a mind trick?"

"Because, my dear. My talent is sensing mental gifts in others. No one else there had so much as a whiff in that room. Dead heads, all of them."

"Huh." Max seemed to be mulling that over, sitting back in his chair. "So what the hell am I going to do when I have to go back there?"

"I have no idea. Let me check with some friends of mine who, erm, specialize in such things."

"Do you really expect me to believe in dead people coming back to talk to their living relations?" Max asked, eyes wide. He seemed utterly appalled.

"Why not? You're a man who can manipulate objects with his mind. How can you credit that and not spiritual energy? It's all electrical impulses, just like Galvani's frog."

When Max simply stared, Andrew sighed. "Italian scientist. He discovered that a dead frog's leg twitched when electricity was applied. We all have such conductors in our bodies."

"What does that have to do with anything?" Max waved a hand, clearly frustrated, and a breeze from nowhere ruffled Andrew's hair.

"Careful, lad. I come here often and I will not be embarrassed by your lack of control."

"My lack of—" Max made to stand, but Andrew grabbed his wrist, holding him fast.

"Sit down, boy. Your food is about to arrive."

Max's butt met the bench with a thump. He stared at Andrew, mouth hanging open.

He smiled. While he had mentioned his ability to sense psychic talent, he might have forgotten to mention his skill in sensing when someone was about to engage their mental capability and dampening it.

"Who are you?" Max asked in a hushed tone.

The food arrived before he could answer, though his only words would have been Andrew Meechum. Simply an ex-soldier who was lucky enough to have good friends who had been able to help him back into the world after the darkest time of his life.

The schnitzel was too crisp and perfect, the apples and cabbage too savory to waste time on explanations. The crusty, rustic bread was the perfect compliment.

They ate in silence, and when they finished the strudel Hilda brought them, they sat back, eyeing one another.

"I have to go," Max said. "You'll speak with your friend?"

Hope sprang up anew. That was an invitation to contact Max again. "I will. Give me your direction and I shall contact you when I know more."

"No." The flat refusal caught him off guard. "I will stop by your club. Which is it?"

He pondered that for a moment. He did belong to more than one, though he never frequented the other. Finally, he pulled a case for calling cards out of his pocket so he could withdraw a card for Club Raven. "I can be reached from this place by runner at any time, day or night. Please call upon me if you need me for whatever reason."

"Thank you." Max took the card and tucked it into the watch pocket of his waistcoat. "And thank you for lunch, Mr. Meechum." He rose, nodding to Andrew.

"Andrew, Max. Remember that. Very few of my club members would know me as Meechum."

"Yes." Max didn't call him by name, but he did stop on the way out of the door to look back and lift a hand in a wave.

Andrew thought perhaps that was progress.

Max ducked into the boarding house where he slept, hoping to avoid the notice of some of the rougher element, who would demand a "toll" for allowing him to pass to his third-floor room. Luckily, he missed them all, and he made his way to 307, pulling out his key from where he wore it on a chain around his neck. He unlocked the door, glancing up with dread when he saw a shadow fall over his feet.

"Busy day, Max?"

Relief made him smile. "Indeed, Flora. You?"

"Oh, you know." She lifted a shoulder, her shawl slipping to show the frilly strap of her chemise below. "Lightly come, lightly go."

He knew Mrs. Casey didn't allow the ladies of the night to ply their trade in her house, but she did rent to many of them. Flora worked in a brothel rather than walking the streets, but she refused to live at her place of business, asserting that she was no prisoner.

"As long as it was easy," Max teased, and Flora chuckled warmly.

"Would you like a nip?" She held up her hand, showing Max a bottle of sherry.

"Oh, not today, thank you. I've just had an enormous luncheon."

"Did you now?" She raked him over with an appraising look. "From one of those séance clients?"

"After a fashion. If I go again I'll bring you back my strudel."

Her bright brown eyes lit up. "Was it apple?"

"It was. I'll try to bring some." Not that he had any intention of ever having a meal with Andrew Meechum ever again, let alone wasting his strudel, but he could definitely buy Flora a treat with what he'd been paid.

He let himself into his room and waved Flora away, then closed and locked the door. He put his valise under the bed. He would need to put some new supplies inside it, but for now he wanted to wash up and stretch out on the bed, where he did his best thinking.

He stripped off his clothes and poured brackish water from the pitcher into the basin. For a nickel he could get fresh, but Max only spent the money when his water ran out entirely.

Max washed quickly before slipping between the sheets, the fresh ticking he'd received a few days before smelling like home.

His mother had made Max and his brother stuff mattresses with hay several times a year, and while his arms would be raw after, the ticking protected the rest of him from the stuff. He slept best when it was fresh.

He thought about his day, from the séance to his luncheon. Max imagined the Calloways both thought it was successful. The wife because she felt a connection to her child, the husband because he had put on a good show.

Max rather thought the whole thing was a disaster.

Andrew was even more worrisome. Devastatingly attractive, far too smart for his own good, and seemingly determined to insinuate himself into Max's life, Andrew Meechum could be his ruination.

Especially since Max had no desire to run from the man deep down in his heart.

He turned over, drawing the covers up around his head to block out the fact that sullen daylight still worked its way around the curtains. Max wanted to escape he whole world, and sleep was the best way to do that; he'd learned that from his mother. Luckily he didn't need laudanum like she had to doze off.

He yawned, then closed his eyes, ready to put Andrew Meechum out of his mind. No matter how attractive or interesting the man was, Max wasn't going to pursue it.

When he shut his eyes all he saw was blond hair and blue eyes with the most intriguing lines around them, so he shook his head, trying to squeeze out the vision. He finally settled on counting backwards from a thousand, which was guaranteed to put him to sleep.

He lay there, breathing, and a rustling sound began to intrude on his rest. Mice were common at the boarding house; too many people kept food in their rooms. He cracked one eye open to look. He kept a small piece of wood next to the bed stand to toss at rodents.

Instead of a mouse, a little girl sat beside his bed on the floor, holding a doll in her lap. He started upright, his heart pounding.

"Who— how did you get in here?"

She didn't answer. She did lift the doll away from her chest to show it to him, and he saw the cameo attached to the collar of her dress.

The Calloway cameo.

"Oh, God. Who are you?"

She smiled, her lips splitting open, her teeth beginning to show through. As she lifted the doll up high, it began to crack right across the face, the porcelain pitting with hairline fractures. When he looked back at the girl, her face was doing the same thing, breaking apart like an outré egg.

A high, thin noise escaped him and he scrambled back, his legs tangling in the covers. "No!"

His shout woke him, and Max sat up, glancing around wildly, his heart pounding. No little girl.

Oh, God.

He listened to his pulse thunder in his ears and he wondered if he should go tomorrow to Andrew Meechum's club and ask him to hurry his investigation. This seemed to be getting serious.

Chapter Four

D o you have a moment, Giles?"

The archivist cum historian at Club Raven peered through his spectacles at Andrew, looking like nothing so much as an owl. He was sat in front of some giant tome, turning pages gently.

"Of course, Andrew! Come in, come in."

"Thank you." He entered the room fully, the scent of leather and paper unmistakable. "I have some questions for you."

"Sit down, then." Giles reached out to move a pile of papers from a dusty chair.

"Thank you." Andrew brushed lint off his trouser leg. "There's a young man I've been working with. A mind-mover who does fake séances."

"Delightful." Giles glanced over the top of glasses. "You must like him."

"Why do you say that?" His pulse speeded.

"Because you didn't simply expose him as a fraud and move on."

Andrew smiled slightly. Sometimes they all forgot how perceptive Giles could be. "Yes, well, he does intrigue me."

"I see. So, what do you need from me?"

"I attended a séance he performed and I think we might have had a visit from a spirit."

Giles leaned forward, hands on his knees. "Do you really think so? Why?"

Andrew explained the orb movement and the cameo. "Max swears he had nothing to do with either."

"Extraordinary. Is there any chance I may visit this home?" Giles had begun to vibrate.

"I can see what they say."

"A personal investigation is always better," Giles told him.

"I see. So you think it could be real, this ghost?"

"Certainly. Get me into that house." Giles' eyes took on the glow of intellectual fervor.

"I shall send a note today." He'd never seen Giles so excited. Andrew was amused as hell. "In the meantime, do I need to worry about young Max being safe?"

"I shouldn't think so if the spirit is tied to the house. Ask him if he's had any further contact." Giles winked. "That way you can see him again."

"Good idea. If I had his direction. He said he would find me here."

"Ah. Cagey." Giles nodded. "When you see him, ask. This information will help my determination."

"Done." Andrew stood. "Thank you, my friend."

Giles followed him to the door. "Thank you! How stimulating."

He shook his head before making his way back downstairs to the billiard room, seeking distraction. He had done his due diligence…

"Oh! Pardon me." He hailed one of the uniformed attendants. He knew the servants in the private area well, but these lads came and went. "A pen and ink, please?"

"Yes, sir. Of course." The lad whirled away, returning moments later with a lap style writing desk.

"Thank you." He would dash off that note to Calloway, then avail himself of the billiard tables and, hopefully, some friends' goodwill.

He hated waiting, but that was all Andrew could do for now.

Max stood on the steps of the Club Raven, shifting from foot to foot.

He wore his best suit, but he knew from watching members come and go that his brown tweed left him woefully underdressed. Still, he'd waited three days to find Andrew, and he hadn't slept a wink in all of them.

The little girl kept appearing, and he needed help. Max was beginning to wonder if he was asleep and dreaming all the time now, or if he was awake.

He finally took a deep breath, steeling himself, before knocking.

A uniformed young man answered the door, his expression carefully blank. "Yes?"

"I—" Max cleared his throat. "I need to leave a message for Andrew Meechum. He said you could send a runner."

"Mr. Meechum arrived not long ago for luncheon. Please come in. You may want to speak to him yourself."

He entered the grand hall, his footsteps echoing on the stone floor.

"Wait here, if you please," the man said before gliding away.

He waited, staring curiously at everything. The grand entry echoed, a huge chandelier hung with crystal and some leather couches dominating the space. The sound of voices reached him, but they were muted as if they came from deep in the bowels of the club.

Andrew joined him a few minutes later, and thankfully he was dressed casually in a pair of buff wool trousers and a dark blue vest and coat. A morning suit, which made Max breathe easier.

"Max!" Andrew bypassed his politely outstretched hands in order to embrace him.

Max went stiff, his whole body on alert. Meechum was far too dangerous to his equilibrium to allow such liberties.

"Just in time for luncheon," Meechum said. "Julian asked for roast with gravy and Yorkshire pudding. I hope you'll stay."

"Oh, I'm not sure..."

"I am." Meechum took his arm, tucking his hand into the crook of Meechum's elbow. "I need a dining companion and I have much to tell you."

"That's why I came," Max said, letting Meechum's momentum carry him around a cavernous main room and into a dining area. The long tables held more crystal and silver than he'd ever seen in his life, and he felt like a country mouse being dragged into a rich cat's corner.

"Is it?" Meechum steered him to a chair. "Has something happened?"

"I'm having dreams." He lowered his voice. "About the girl. The Calloway daughter."

"Really? How fascinating. Did you see the portrait of her at the Calloway home?"

Max frowned. "No, did you?"

"Yes. Now, tell me what you've seen."

"She's young. Maybe eight. Blonde curls, bright blue eyes. She wears a cream-colored dress and the cameo we saw at the séance."

"That could be any of hundreds of children." Still Andrew frowned, didn't he?

"She's not, though. She's the Calloway girl."

"It would seem so, yes." Andrew flagged down a waiter with a lifted finger. "Coffee?"

"Do you have milk?" When the waiter nodded silently, Max smiled. "Milk, please."

"And we'll both have the roast."

"Very good, Mr. Meechum."

Max waited for Andrew to speak. When he didn't, Max sighed. "So? What news?"

"My friend assures me that the spiritual component could be very real. He wants to visit the house."

"Good for him." Max hunched his shoulders. He would prefer never to return to that place, even if the money was some of the best he'd ever made.

"Yes, well, I contacted Mr. Calloway and he will only allow it if you agree to do another séance. His wife is eager to see what you can do now."

"No." Max shook his head. "Whatever it is that happened, the girl is following me now. She's not just at her parents' house."

"Conversely, if you return and we find out what she wants, she will leave you alone."

"You think." Max didn't like this idea at all. How could they be sure that was what would happen?

"Giles is really quite an expert at this. Let him come with us. Do a simple séance. See what happens." Andrew reached out to him, placing one hand over his.

The contact stunned him into stillness. Goosebumps rose on his skin. Good God, what a simple thing to make him so confused.

No one touched him save for his séance attendees when they held his hand. He couldn't afford the physical contact.

This was not the same sort of contact at all. Andrew stared at him, blue eyes full of some emotion Max couldn't name.

He pulled back, his hand tingling. "I— I don't know."

"You don't need to make a decision now." Andrew sat back when their drinks were delivered, his expression shuttered again. Pleasant.

"No. Thank you." He was going to begin babbling any moment, so he clamped his lips shut.

Andrew smiled at someone in passing, the expression fond, and Max felt a surge of jealousy, completely unfounded. This man meant nothing to him, and it was forbidden, what he wanted.

Max cleared his throat. "Explain to me what your friend wants to do?"

"I can have him come down, if you like."

"No." He said it too fast, but he wanted to have Andrew to himself somehow. "No, just tell me."

"Sorry." Andrew gave him a curious glance. "He wants to go with us and attend a séance. He says that's the best method for him to see if the activity is genuine."

"I see. You won't make me do it alone, though."

"Not at all. I will be there the whole way." Andrew's solid assurance eased him some.

"Then I'll do it." Max said it in a rush, but he meant it. He needed the apparition of the little girl to leave him be, and he needed to see Andrew Meechum again.

The waiter returned with a tray on wheels. When he lifted silver domes off their plates Max drooled. The roast smelled like heaven, making him think of Sunday dinners he'd eaten as a child. The little breads they called Yorkshire puddings had a crisp, delicate look, and he could hardly wait to fill them with gravy.

"Looks delightful, doesn't it?"

"It does. Smells better." Max waited politely for the plates to land before them, and for Andrew to cut a bite, before digging in with enthusiasm. He must admit he ate better with Meechum than he had on his own for years.

"Oh, goodness." Andrew ate heartily, a rare thing among those who lodged where Max did.

Drunkards ate little.

Max ate until he didn't think he could bear anymore. Then their waiter brought spice cake with a sugary glaze. Oh, he loved spice cake with nuts. "This is my favorite cake."

"Is it? Mine is a pound cake with lemon," Andrew said. "The spice cake here is worth it, however."

"I hope so." He eyed it, trying to determine how much to eat based on how full his belly was. One bite had him throwing caution to the wind and eating it all, then pondering asking for another.

"The kitchen always makes enough to last for several days, hmm? We can have another piece later."

"Oh, no." Max pushed away the empty plate. "I must leave

soon." Should he get the other piece anyway? For Flora?

"Really? Why?" Andrew frowned slightly, the barest line appearing between his eyebrows. "Do you have another séance? A social engagement?"

"No, nothing like that."

"Laundry? Bathing day?" Now Andrew was clearly teasing, the light in those blue eyes intimate and laughing.

"No. No. I am not a member here."

"You are my guest. I love billiards. Do you play?"

"Not since my youth."

Andrew snorted. "As if the bloom is off you. Hardly, Max."

"You can't be much older than me!" He was no child to be made sport of.

"I think you underestimate the years of experience I have." Andrew rose. "Come along, Max. I need to work off luncheon."

His heart raced at the words, but he knew full well Andrew meant billiards, so he felt ridiculous. A tiny bit of desire tucked away for contemplation later never hurt anyone.

The billiard room left Max speechless. Three billiard tables sat in splendor at one end of a long common room, all with plenty of space about them to shoot. Two men played at one table, but the others were empty.

"Mind if we join you, gents?" Andrew asked, and both men nodded easily.

"As long as you know we're playing for favors and not money." The older man, a handsome gent with silver hair Max thought was premature, smiled, looking a bit like a wolf.

Predatory.

"Of course you are."

The younger fellow blushed a rosy hue, but only smiled, lifting his chin at Max.

"This is Max…" Andrew glanced at him, eyebrow rising.

"Bellame. Max Bellame."

"Pleasure. Lionel James." The older man held out a hand to shake. "And this is Horace Little."

"How do you do?" Max fell back on the manners his genteel mother had ingrained in him from a young age.

"Hello." Horace shook hands with him as well. "It's great to see Mr. Meechum with a friend."

"Um. Yes." He tried for a smile, but Andrew simply laughed.

"You mean rather than dominating Lionel's attention, Little?"

"Just so!" Horace smiled brightly.

Max wasn't sure what any of that meant, so he racked balls and chalked a cue instead of joining the conversation. When Andrew walked close, he murmured, "I cannot play for money, Andrew."

"I wouldn't ask you to, Max. You work for your pennies."

"You don't?" Max asked, rather surprised.

"Oh, I oversee some interests for my father. Some banking concerns, a few properties." Something about Andrew's tone told Max not to ask further.

"I see." He didn't, but so be it. He had no inheritance. His very sweet, educated mother had come with a good dowry, but his father had been a ne'er do well descended from French trappers, and had left them high dry more than once.

"I'll let you shoot to see who goes first." Andrew murmured.

"So kind." He bent over the table to make sure it was level, then shot the cue ball toward the opposite rail. He did well, ending close to the rail without touching. Andrew didn't do so well, so Max began with the first carom.

His third shot missed, and he stepped back to allow Andrew a turn.

Andrew passed him, bending to make his shot, and Max glanced away, trying not to look at the way Andrew's trousers stretched over his bottom.

What he saw when he looked toward Lionel and Horace shocked him. Lionel had backed Horace up against the table and was leaning close, kissing the other man's mouth.

He had never seen such a thing in a public place. Never thought to.

"Your go, Max."

Max jumped a good half a foot, his cheeks on fire.

"Does it bother you?" Andrew asked.

"I don't know how to answer that." Such things were considered immoral and illegal. If he admitted that was what he wanted more than anything, to have a man in that way, what would Andrew think of him?

"I know how I would answer." Andrew nodded at the table, and Max promptly failed his shot.

"How?" Max had to ask.

"It arouses me." Andrew met his gaze head on. "I have been with Lionel. I know how he rewards his lovers."

His mouth went dry as dust, and his cock rose to half-hardness in his trousers. Max stood there, holding his cue stick, and staring.

"I've shocked you," Andrew said with a wry smile on his face.

"I suppose so." Max chuckled. "I guess I've never heard it so baldly stated."

"No? Club Raven is one place we don't have to hide such proclivities, Max."

"Why?" He felt as if that was the only word he still knew how to say.

"Because the members are open to these things. Or we don't become members."

Had Andrew seen something in him, noticed the glances Max couldn't help stealing? Surely not. Max tried not to admit his needs, even to himself. They could get a man killed or jailed.

"I really don't know what you want from me. It's your play, Andrew."

Andrew stared at him for a moment longer. Then he nodded and turned back to the game. "I would feel badly if a guest I brought was uncomfortable."

"No. No, I have no troubles, Andrew. I mean it." Max felt as though it was important to say it. "It confuses me. Worries me as to what you think of me."

"Never worry that I would think less of you no matter how you feel," Andrew said. "Though confused is good enough for me right now."

A soft moan sounded behind them, and Max tried not to turn, not to look. He had to sneak at least a glance, and his heart jumped in his chest. Lionel had a hand fully down the front of Horace's trousers.

"Lionel." Andrew said it softly, but to immediate effect.

Lionel raised his head, staring at Andrew. Whatever passed between them, it had Lionel nodding and taking Horace by the hand. "Come along, pet. We need to find a more private area."

"Better," Andrew murmured. "The billiard room is in a public area. They were indiscreet."

"Is it acceptable to be indiscreet in the private areas?"

Andrew moved past him to make his next shot, his voice low and intimate when he said, "Oh, yes."

"Oh." His cock did not subside. Not one bit. In fact, he thought it rose higher, striving to make a tent in his fly.

Andrew's soft chuckle made him want to run, but his feet wouldn't move. He was drawn so strongly to Andrew, and knowing Andrew had taken male lovers made Max even more intrigued.

"I missed." Andrew brushed by him again, one hand touching Max's wrist, fingers trailing gently over the patch of bare skin there.

Max gasped, his nipples hardening, gooseflesh rising along his arms. What on earth was he doing? Perhaps it was the spice cake. Did they put something in it? The thought had him laughing out loud, his fancy too much to bear.

"What is it?" Andrew asked.

"My ridiculous ideas. Where are we at score? Nine?"

"Eight." Andrew nodded at the table, and Max bent to make his shot, not really even looking.

"Wait. Let me show you." Andrew sidled up behind him, one

hand on his lower back. Then Andrew leaned over him, molding that long, lean form to his back and buttocks.

Max caught his breath, forgetting how to let it out. Oh, God in heaven that felt good. So good. He blinked, sweat beading on his upper lip while Andrew lined up his cue stick.

"There, you see?" Andrew's low voice sounded just behind his ear, the warm puff of air making him shiver.

"No. I mean, I need you to show me. More explicitly."

The puff of breath turned into a chuckle. "Of course. You see, if you line it up here." Andrew helped him fix his cue on a point. "Then you can rebound here and here."

"I do see." With Andrew's help, Max made the shot. He also leaned a little with his mind moving to keep the ball on target.

"I felt that, Max. No cheating."

"I wasn't. I was keeping things even. You're very distracting."

"I do try." Andrew backed away, but not before Max felt the hard press of Andrew's cock against his hip.

He lost the ability to think clearly, his body on fire. His cock was fully hard now, aching. He had no idea what to do, so he hid behind the table.

"Are you well, Max?" Andrew asked, eyes like blue fire, watching him closely.

"No. I'm having wicked thoughts."

"So am I." Andrew's gaze traveled down to his button placket.

"Stop." His ears were going to catch fire, they were so hot. "It's unseemly at best."

"Oh, Max. I am nothing if not inappropriate." Andrew moved close enough for their bodies to brush, for him to smell sandalwood and citrus over Andrew's clean, masculine musk. "Let me show you how much."

He wanted to step back, but Max found that he'd stepped forward instead, pressing against Andrew's chest. "Yes. Please." A great spirit of recklessness possessed him, made him do things he would otherwise shy from.

Andrew's smile widened, and he took Max's hand, discarding the pool cue in favor of tugging him out of the room, much like Lionel had done with Horace earlier.

Max didn't ask where they were going. He simply followed, his need riding him, pushing him to see how far this all would go.

They made their way to a grand staircase, then followed it up to the second floor, where Andrew took him to a well-appointed room with a chaise lounge, a bed, and a card table with chairs.

"So is this a Molly House?" Max asked.

"Not exactly, no. But members do have a safe place to enjoy one another."

Max laughed, turning in a full circle. "Well, it's nicer than my boarding house."

"And far more intimate than my mausoleum of a home." Andrew reached for him, callused fingers tugging at his clothing.

Max let it happen, moving close when Andrew grabbed his hips and pulled. They pressed together from chest to knees, which stole Max's breath right away.

When Andrew kissed him, though, the world stood still.

Max opened up and let Andrew in, the contact rough and hot and not at all genteel and sweet. He'd expected a slow seduction from this urbane man, but he was receiving a full scale attack to his senses. This was an all-out, well-planned offensive from an experienced soldier.

Andrew pushed him backward until his legs hit the bed, and Max jerked to a halt, his body jolted by the impact. Then Andrew began working on his clothing, his jacket and tie flying one way, his collar and shirt the other.

He tried to undo Andrew's tie, but the knot confounded his fingers. He pulled it free at long last, flinging it down in frustration.

Andrew laughed. "Impatient?"

"I want to see you like you see me."

"Oh, sweet man, I doubt that's possible." Still, Andrew

obligingly stripped off collar and jacket and shirt. Now they both wore only trousers and shoes.

As if reading his mind, Andrew knelt to help remove Max's shoes and socks, the touches tickling his skin. His toes curled up, and Max thought no one had touched him thus since perhaps his nanny, who was long gone by the time he was two.

Then Andrew started on the buttons of Max's fly, which was when he forgot how to breathe. He watched that blond head bob before him, those clever hands work his fly open. Then Andrew pulled down Max's pants, leaving him bare naked, his cock springing up to stand proud and hard.

"Mmm. Lovely." Andrew stared right at his prick, licking those well-shaped lips. No one had ever stared so at his privates, and it was a freeing experience.

"I— Thank you." Max had to laugh, his nerves getting the better of him.

"I mean it. Are you nervous, Max?"

"I hardly know you." That was honest enough, even though he felt Andrew would not harm him.

"Sometimes that adds spice." Andrew titled his shining head and licked Max from base to tip.

He shouted, then clapped a hand over his mouth. He didn't want to attract attention from the other rooms.

"This is no boarding house, Max. You can make all the noise you like."

He doubted that. Max was already pretty loud.

Then Andrew gripped his cock by the base and sucked him in, lips sealing halfway down his shaft.

He rose up on his toes, his hips pushing forward, his muscles clenching. He couldn't breathe, couldn't stop the motion of his body as he rocked back and forth.

Andrew pressed one hand, palm up, against his balls, rolling them to and fro. The sensation sent lightning shooting up his spine to explode like a cloudburst in his brain.

He made this noise, somewhere between a whine and a

grunt. Max wasn't going to last. He'd never experienced this. A private place. The undivided attention of a stunning man.

No, he'd never felt anything as close to heaven as Andrew Meechum's mouth.

When Andrew pressed one questing finger against the skin behind his balls, dangerously close to his most secret entrance, Max lost himself. He spent into Andrew's mouth, his whole body jerking and dancing against the plush bed.

He panted, hanging there, not sure what to do or say.

Andrew stood, pressing him back to kiss his mouth, letting him taste himself. Scandalized, he opened up and let Andrew in, tongue rubbing against his.

Max reached up to grip Andrew's wide shoulders, the feel of bare skin shocking him because he'd forgotten that he'd managed to remove those layers of Andrew's clothes.

"Oh, sweet. I want to fuck you."

Max pushed Andrew away, staring. "What?"

"Is it too soon?" Andrew laughed, the sound rueful. "Your hand, then."

"No, I mean what did you mean?"

"You know what a Molly House is but you have no idea how two men fuck?" Andrew asked.

His cheeks heated painfully, and any lingering stiffness left his prick. "Don't laugh at me."

"I'm not. I'm charmed by you." Andrew stepped forward to place a hand on his cheek.

"Are you?" Uncertain, he looked at Andrew from under his lashes.

"Can you tell?" Reaching down with the other hand, Andrew caught Max's wrist, moving him until his palm pressed to the hard bulge in Andrew's trousers.

"Goodness." He explored blindly, staring into Andrew's blue eyes. The heat lurking beneath the cloth shouldn't shock him, but it did. "Yes."

Andrew helped him, unbuttoning buttons and moving

cloth until Max touched flesh. He stroked with three fingers, testing the length and hardness of Andrew's shaft, which was impressive. He circled it with his fingers and thumb, rubbing as he would rub himself.

Moaning, Andrew rocked into his touch. "Yes. Just like that, Max. Harder, though."

Max wasn't ready for harder; he wanted a slow, steady learning of Andrew's body. Still, he understood. Andrew had taken the time and effort to give him pleasure untold. Now Andrew was ready for his own little death.

Max moved faster, jerking his hand up and down Andrew's cock. Now he stared down at where their skin met, the deep red of Andrew's cockhead appearing and disappearing against the edge of his palm. Fascinating.

He watched, and Andrew rode his hand, panting, finally reaching down to squeeze his hand around that rigid length far more firmly than Max would have dared.

The pressure seemed to be exactly what Andrew needed, because he grunted, body bucking, and hot seed spilled over Max's fingers. He rubbed his hand up and down, massaging the issue into Andrew's skin, watching every moment.

"Mmm. Much better, Max." Andrew laughed, the sound as far from mean as he could imagine. "I suggest we do it all again, this time with both of us on the bed."

"I—" Max broke off his instinctive protest. Well, why not? This would be his only chance, he imagined. Why shouldn't he enjoy the sins of the flesh with this beautiful man while he could?

So he nodded, pushing himself all the way up on the bed. "I think that sounds a fine idea."

Andrew climbed up on the bed with him, hands on his thighs. "So do I, Max. So do I."

Chapter Five

Andrew woke in the wee hours before dawn, and he knew Max had gone.

They had indulged most of the day in all of the best sins: sex and whiskey and rich food. He had watched Max sleep for a long while, not willing to let Max slip away, which he knew would happen as soon as he slept.

He'd been right.

He sighed, rolling to his back to stretch his arms up over his head. What to do with Max? He was hardly ready to let the lad go.

Maybe next time he would tie Max to the bed.

A soft knock on the door had him springing out of bed, thinking perhaps Max had been unable to take the final step of leaving the club. Sometimes the Raven did work against people.

"Oh, Lionel."

"You needn't sound so disappointed, old friend." Lionel's gently mocking expression showed how his expectation had been in clear evidence.

Andrew laughed, stepping back to allow Lionel to enter the room. "Sorry. I was just abandoned, and hoped he had changed his mind."

"Alas, no. He left an hour or more ago." Lionel lit a lamp, then turned to stare at him critically, taking in every detail of his no doubt disheveled appearance. "You're quite taken with him."

"Are you jealous?" Andrew felt no need to cover up, sprawling on the bed so he could peer at Lionel.

"A bit." The admission surprised him. "I count on you to be

my equal in all things, Andrew. To know you might be serious about him means I will lose footing with you."

"Now you're being absurd." He would always have a deep care for Lionel. Theirs was not a love match and never had been, but he adored this man.

Lionel smiled faintly. "It's good that you think so, my dear."

"Stop it." Andrew sighed. "So you saw him leave?"

"I did. He was all aflutter. Quite in turmoil. You confuse him. Honestly, you would think you asked for far more than a fuck."

He shot Lionel a dark look. "Sometimes I think you harbor more than empathy in that dark mind of yours."

"He was thinking loud enough I'm sure Koni heard him, even, all the way up in his aerie."

Andrew shivered. Koni was a red Indian, and he moved about the club like a spirit, his impassive face impossible to read. He made Andrew wickedly uncomfortable.

"At any rate, if you still want that fuck…" Lionel raised a dark brow, waiting.

"What happened to the young man you had? Horace?" He thought certain Horace had intended wickedness.

"Ah, he was a bit of a bore." Lionel stood, then stripped off his linen shirt.

Andrew knew it was probably unwise to allow Lionel in when Max had just gone, but he also knew he had rarely turned down his friend when he was in need. He held out a hand and, after he divested himself of his trousers, Lionel joined him on the bed.

They settled easily together, their bodies knowing the shape of one another.

"Tell me what's wrong, Lionel."

Lionel chuckled, lips only inches from his. "Nothing you can't take away, Andrew. Kiss me."

He did just that, pressing his lips to Lionel's, the fire in his belly a slow, familiar thing with his friend. Not like the quick flash Max engendered in him, but heated all the same. A tiny guilt pinged at him, but he had a feeling Max meant to be gone for good. At least that was what he told himself.

When it came time, it was Lionel inside him as it always was, his friend having taught him everything he knew about submitting to another's will.

Now it was his turn to pass those lessons along to someone else.

Max sat with the other renters at Mrs. Casey's eating porridge for breakfast and trying to decide what to do.

Reason told him to pack up and move on as he had every time things got sticky. Maybe he would head west. Chicago was booming…

The irrational side of him ached to see Andrew again, perhaps to allow him to do all the things he talked about doing. The long, explicit explanation had floored him.

He pushed the spoon from bowl to mouth mechanically, ignoring as best he could the uncouth slurping going on around him. Mrs. Casey served decent food for a nickel or a dime, depending on the meal, and Max couldn't complain, though he did wonder if they served breakfast at Club Raven.

On the good side, a night spent with Andrew seemed to have cured him of visitation from the little girl. He had not seen or dreamed of her last night at all.

"Max." Mrs. Casey bustled over, filling his coffee. "This came for you." She placed a folded sheet of paper by his bowl. "Said to give it to you right away."

"Thank you." He stared at it. What did Andrew's handwriting look like?

He opened the note, and was disappointed. The Calloways. They asked his attendance this afternoon to discuss the best course of action. The lady of the house was having bad dreams. Intensely bad, apparently. Not just about Charlotte, but her other dead children as well.

Damnation.

He would stop by the Calloway house after breakfast, he supposed. Like it or not, he had unleashed something inside that house. It was his duty to quash it. He would have no more incidents like the fire. No, he would never be responsible again for someone's very real agony.

He sighed, pushing aside his bowl. Looked like he needed to send another message to Andrew Meechum. He'd promised not to go back to the Calloways without Andrew and his friend.

He left his nickel for Mrs. Casey, knowing no one would ever take it from her dining room. Then he walked to the front hall, where Mrs. Casey kept writing implements and paper. For a price, naturally. He slipped a dime into the lock box and took a piece of paper. The pen needed a new nib, but the ink was fine and dark.

"Andrew. The Calloways want me to attend them at two pm today. Can you be there with your friend in tow? Max."

Keeping it simple and unemotional seemed best.

"Mrs. Casey?" He knocked softly on her office door. The room had been a small library at one time when the house had been a single home.

"Well, what is it?"

Max pulled out one last dime, which left him very little without breaking the large bills the Calloways had given him. He would stop and cash for smaller bills and coins today. "Can you have this delivered to the Club Raven?" He gave her the direction.

"Of course." She held out her hand, and he gave her the dime first, then the envelope.

"It's rather urgent."

"I'll send my nephew now."

"Thank you, ma'am."

When she left him, Max sighed. Back upstairs to collect his things. He needed more glass orbs, but he thought perhaps it was best to leave them behind this time anyway. The silly thing had proven dangerous at the Calloway home.

He packed, his mind racing like a mouse in a grain mill. He should leave. Just get out of town. Move on. That was what he was good at. He knew he had a responsibility, but he wanted to get away. Max shook with the need, in fact.

He stared at his hands, willing them to still. "I am not a coward, and I will not leave another family with a problem they cannot solve."

He squared his shoulders. Off he went to the Calloways' home by way of a shop to buy some sage. He could only hope Andrew was available to meet him there.

Chapter Six

The message came just about the time Andrew was about to give into boredom and seek out someone to play billiards with him. He was haunting Club Raven and he knew it; he should go home and do some work on his father's accounts. He was waiting for the next encounter with Max, which was probably ridiculous.

Or so he thought, until the message came. A lad brought it to him, a tiny scuffle with the door attendant making Andrew laugh aloud. "Mrs. Casey says I was to bring this right to you, sir. If you're Andrew Meechum."

"I am." He pulled a coin from his pocket, the lad's eyes going huge and round at the sight of it. "Thank you."

"Thank you, sir!" The boy ran away, right out the front door. He imagined the Raven was… unnerving for children who saw and heard things adults had long forgotten existed.

Andrew opened the missive, which was brief, but made his heart pound anyway. He jumped to his feet, running up the main stairs to the second floor. "Giles! Giles, are you about?"

Giles popped out of a hidden door, seeming to come out of thin air. "I am always about. What are you shouting for?"

"That house you wished to examine. The Calloway home?"

Giles nodded, blinking owlishly behind his spectacles. "What about it?"

"They want us to come now."

Giles smiled, lips curving wickedly. "Really? How diverting! Daniel!"

The blind servant who seemed to be everywhere appeared,

much like Giles had only moments before. "Yes, Mr. Giles?"

"My bag, please. The one I use for investigations. And my coat, if you please. Andrew and I are off on an adventure."

"Very good, sir."

Daniel ducked back into the wall, it seemed, and returned in no time, a carpet bag and coat in hand. "Shall I inform the owners?"

"Yes, please. I should only be a few hours."

"Are you chained to the archives, then?" Andrew asked on the way down the stairs. He would stop at coat check to retrieve his jacket, as well.

"Not exactly," Giles hedged. "They do worry when I'm away. I do rarely leave the club, you see."

"Ah." No, Andrew didn't see, but that hardly mattered. There were things about Club Raven that he didn't question. Easier on a man's mind that way.

Giles glanced around curiously as they made their way out into the street. "Gracious, look how everything has grown."

Andrew gave him a sidelong glance. "You really need to get out more."

"Undoubtedly. So busy! All these people! Look at that ridiculous hat!" Giles indicated a middle-aged matron, who drew her skirts away from them in affront.

Andrew shook his head, but let it go, smiling faintly. Max had called for his help, had asked him to come to the Calloway house.

His body tightened, and he tried hard to remember he was in public.

"You're very attached already," Giles said.

"I am. Is that bad? I have no doubt it will end poorly, but caution is boring."

Giles laughed, the sound delighted. "Indeed. Good for you, my friend. So, remind me about this family."

"Father. Mother. Lost half a dozen children to disease."

"Not to the war?"

"Only one, and he lied about his age to get in. They were all young."

"Sad." Giles pulled a face. "You said the mother was the one desperate to communicate."

"Yes. She's a believer. The husband is indulgent. Loves that Max has produced results because it cheers up his wife. Sad, really."

"Hope is the most terrible of all emotions," Giles agreed. "I much prefer faith."

"I did not take you as a religious man, Giles."

Giles gave him an arch look. "Faith and religion are mutually exclusive."

He hooted. "I suppose they are at that."

"What is our tack today, then? Our pretense for me coming in?"

"Mentor? You can be the one teaching Max to do séances. There just to make sure he didn't make a terrible mistake."

"Oh, I like it." Giles nodded, apparently pleased.

"Good. The simpler the better."

"Yes. The fewer lies one must remember, the fewer mistakes one makes." Giles put a hand on his arm. "We turn here."

Andrew looked at the street sign. "So we do. You're rather magical, Giles."

"I am!" Giles led the way, moving right to the Calloways' home with no further direction. Amazing.

Max met them at the door, his sober face tilting toward a smile. "Andrew."

"Max. Giles was so pleased that you swallowed your pride and asked for your mentor's help, finally."

Max's eyes widened. "Yes, well, you know how proud I am. Thank you for coming, Giles."

"Not a problem at all, my lad." Giles stepped past Max into the house, where Mr. Calloway stood. No one else inhabited the foyer, so Andrew assumed the men were to have a serious talk before joining the rest of the family.

"Giles Leonne, sir, at your service." Giles shook hands with Mr. Calloway, his demeanor suddenly quite professional.

"Good, good," Calloway jerked his head. "All here then, so let's retire to my study."

Max nodded easily. "Naturally."

The four of them trooped across the main hall, past the stairs, and down a small corridor. The study was a small room smelling of leather and brandy, and Andrew was surprised to find it quite pleasant.

They all took a seat and, without asking, Calloway poured them all a brandy.

"Early in the day for a serious spirit," Andrew said carefully.

Calloway's face clouded up like an impending storm. "This nonsense is beginning to cause troubles, gentlemen. My wife is not sleeping. That damned cameo keeps popping up no matter where I hide it. She's having terrible dreams." Calloway leveled a finger at Max. "Make it stop."

Max looked at Andrew, eyes wide, but Giles stepped right in. "Max called me in because I have been his teacher in the art of mediumship. I told him to allow me to observe and make a determination of the best course of action."

"Observe what? Surely you don't mean another damned séance?" Calloway asked. "What if another dead child shows up?"

"I assure you, Mr. Calloway. I can deal with any eventuality."

Max blinked, staring at Giles with a sort of wonder that made a hard spurt of jealousy rise up in Andrew's chest.

Andrew cleared his throat. "Giles is an expert in the field. Max is a wonderful medium, but rogue spirits are not normal for him."

"Hrm. Well." There was much throat clearing and mumbling before Calloway tossed back his brandy, then smoothed one hand down his tie. "Let me speak to my family. In the meantime, enjoy your brandy, gents."

Giles immediately set his drink aside, then leveled a stare at

Max. "I'll fix this for you, lad, but then you have a decision to make."

Max stared back, and Andrew was proud of his gumption. "I do?"

"Mmm. We'll discuss it over dinner. The three of us," Giles added, nodding at Andrew.

His shoulders relaxed. Good. That was good. He wasn't going to share Max with anyone. Well, not for a long while, and only then if he and Max both agreed to play together.

Max shook his head. "I make no promises. I could have left town on the next stage. Or even the train. I chose to stay and help."

"You are plucky, I'll give you that." Giles rose, then tugged his bag up onto the chair. He opened it so he could rummage through the contents. He pulled out first a wall thermometer, then what looked like a miniature wind gauge. The device would sit on a table and turn with little paper sails if there was a strong draft.

"While you two participate in the séance, I will be gathering data," Giles said.

Even Andrew had to stare. "How very…"

"Thorough," Max finished for Andrew. "I thought you said everyone at this club of yours had talents like mine."

Giles looked at Max over his spectacles, the light gleaming off them, making his eyes appear golden. "Oh, my dear. I have far more talent than you do. Do not underestimate me."

Andrew actually sat back in his chair, the burst of power coming from Giles shocking him. Andrew was used to tiny pinpricks of light in a dark forest of people. Giles was a beacon.

Max's eyes widened as well. "Fine."

Giles grinned, all teeth. "Fine."

"Good." Andrew clapped his hands. "Glad that's all settled."

Calloway popped back into the room. "My wife is willing to participate. She has sent a message to her sister and to the children's old nanny. They should arrive in half an hour or so.

If you're hungry there's meats and cheeses and bread in the kitchen."

"Oh, excellent," Giles said. "I am a bit peckish." He rose up and followed Calloway out.

Max looked at Andrew, his eyes a bit wild. "He's—"

"A force of nature. Yes." Andrew chuckled. "Have you eaten?"

"I have, yes. I should set up the parlor." Max fiddled with the clasp of his bag, not quite meeting Andrew's eyes. A breeze ruffled his hair.

"Steady, love. I'll help." Andrew glanced at the door before striding over to Max to grasp his upper arms and yank him close for a kiss.

Max gasped, then kissed him back with equal fervor, lips opening to let him in. Max's bag thudded to the floor, those hands clutched Andrew's shoulders, keeping them close together.

When they broke for air, he stared deep into Max's eyes. "You left me."

"You scare me," Max murmured. "I cannot afford to care about anyone more than I do about my well-being."

A huge swell of satisfaction rolled through Andrew. Max cared for him. Wanted him.

"There's nothing to be afraid of, Max."

"Of course there is." Max smiled, the expression wry.

"Well, I happen to think you're wrong."

"You're both idiots." Giles returned with a heaping plate of food. "Just look at these pickles. So adorable."

"You are an odd duck, Giles. Max needs to set up." He stepped back from Max, but they would finish this later.

"Of course he does." Giles waved a hand languidly. "Go do your business, young mentee."

Max glanced back and forth between them, clearly amused, then shook his head. "I'll be in the parlor."

"We'll be out soon." Andrew frowned at Giles, who waved a pickle in the air.

"Indubitably."

Once Max had grabbed his bag and left the room, Andrew turned on Giles. "What on earth are you about?"

"Teasing you. It's glorious. You thought you knew me so well." Giles eyed a tiny sausage before snapping it up viciously.

"I need you to be serious, Giles."

Nodding, Giles popped a sliver of cheese into his mouth. "And I will when needs must call for it. Right now I can play," he said around the cheese.

Andrew had to laugh. He shook his head. "Give me some of that. I'm starving."

"I knew you would be." Giles shared his plate. "I can feel the little girl. She's curious. There are others, too."

"Is she? Why is she still here, do you think? Why are any of them?" Andrew munched a bit of rustic bread with a piece of cheese atop it.

"Because her mother doesn't want her to move on. She should have been buried with that cameo. It was her very favorite thing."

"Ah." He chewed, trying not to speak with his mouth full. "I'll tell Max so he can make that his suggestion. To bury it."

"Indeed." Giles winked, then popped another pickle in his mouth. "I really must speak to Cook. We need more fermented foods."

"Whatever pleases you, Giles."

"Well, that's the idea. We work hard for the club. It needs to work hard for me." Giles smacked his lips, his expression so lecherous that Andrew backed up a step.

"I suppose so." Andrew did work for the Club Raven, but he thought of it as a social club, a place to be with friends like Lionel.

"You're far too cavalier, my friend."

"Mmm." Andrew tried a couple of pickles, and some very salty meat. "Let me go tell Max what to set up."

"Yes, do. I'll be along apace." Giles munched, making happy noises.

Andrew shook his head, but he had to laugh. He made his way to the parlor, where Max was pulling closed curtains and draping the table with a fringed velvet scarf.

"Such a showman," Andrew teased.

Max flushed pink. "It helps set the stage. I think it works. Perhaps better in poorer houses."

"Of course. I was jesting." He grabbed Max's bag. "What else would you like?"

"Candles, if I have any. I need to—" Max's flush deepened. "I need to discuss payment with Mr. Calloway."

"Ah. Remind me to discuss an arrangement with you."

Max's expression turned to stone. "I'm not interested."

"I'm not asking that." He could see Max had no interest in becoming a kept man. "I have a job offer from the Club."

Curiosity crept into Max's eyes. "Later."

"Very well." Andrew inclined his head. "Giles says the girl knows we're here. She's curious. She wants her locket with her; the mother refused to bury it with the child."

Max shuddered, closing his eyes a moment. "I don't want to know how Giles knows this. Ever."

"I don't blame you a bit." Andrew thought perhaps Giles' easy acceptance of spirits was a tad off-putting.

"Are you almost ready?" Mr. Calloway hovered in the doorway, shifting from foot to well-shod foot.

"Nearly," Max said quietly. "I am sorry if anything I did has caused issues, sir, but—"

"Yes, yes. I'll pay you, lad. As we agreed before." Calloway was a canny man. He knew exactly what Max was worries about, and Andrew thought he might even approve.

"Thank you, sir," Max said, evincing convincing gratitude. "I appreciate it very much."

Andrew kept his expression carefully blank. He hated the idea of Max scraping for pennies, but that was the way of things, wasn't it?

Calloway left them, presumably to gather the family, and

Max glanced at Andrew. "I have no orbs or any such devices."

Andrew snorted. "I should think the little miss will put on quite a show. If she doesn't, I say pick this figurine here to smash. It came from a dime store and means nothing to Mrs. Calloway. The mister rather loathes it."

Max squinted at him. "You're as terrifying as Giles. Very well. I'm ready."

"I'll get Giles."

"Be careful." When he glanced at Max, he got a faint smile and a wink. Teasing was a good sign, he thought.

He made his way to the study. "Giles— what the devil are you doing?"

Giles lay on the large chesterfield, his feet up on one leather arm. "I was digesting my meal and communing with the ceiling. Are we ready?"

"We are."

"Good." Giles rose before grabbing his measuring devices. "I shall set up at a smaller table behind you and Max."

"Just try not to distract him unduly. His fine control still needs work."

"I understand." Giles followed him to the parlor. "That one, then?" he asked, nodding at the figurine Andrew and Max had chosen as their prop.

"If needs be, yes."

"Perfect." Giles pulled over a twisted leg table, the screech of the glass ball feet on the wooden floor left bare where the rug did not touch horrendous.

Andrew glared at him, but the family began to file into the room, so now was clearly not the time to argue.

Later.

The Calloways settled around the table Max had set up, and Mr. Calloway moved to sit next to Mrs. Calloway rather than on the other side of Max, leaving that for Andrew, for which he was grateful. He settled in close, grabbing Max's hand once his lover sat and reached for him.

His lover. What an extraordinary thought.

Max shot him a startled glance when their skin touched. Yes. It was as if a tiny lightning bolt had passed between them. They would concentrate now and explore that fire later.

They turned to the center of the table. Max nodded, because everyone was ready, holding hands and watching intently.

"Thank you all for coming together today," Max intoned. "I'm sorry if rousing the spirits in this house have caused a disturbance. Today we will try to ascertain what your daughter wants, what she needs so she can move on."

Andrew felt Max wince, and he would imagine Mrs. Calloway had dug her claws into his hand. She didn't want her daughter's spirit to disappear. No, she wanted them to have tea parties. Too bad little Charlotte was far more intent upon wreaking havoc.

Perhaps that was unfair. He didn't care.

Max cleared his throat. "Focus inward on our circle. Push your breath into it and ask the spirit among us to come forth."

They all drew in breath and let it out as if they were one beast. They all waited, and Andrew was dimly aware of Giles behind them through the sound of the tiny wind machine, flapping away.

The spirit was among them. Andrew wondered if Max knew it.

"Come to us, tell us what you desire," Max droned, seemingly oblivious.

A gust of wind none of them could ignore shot through the room. The curtains at the end of the room never moved. Just their hair and the tablecloth where they sat.

Mrs. Calloway moaned, though Andrew couldn't tell if it was fear or ecstasy.

"We must be quiet so the spirit can speak. Tell us, if you can, are you a daughter of this house?"

A sharp knocking sound answered them, eliciting gasps all around. Andrew had felt the surge of talent come from Max, and he knew his faux medium was giving this his all.

"Yes." Max's voice rose just enough to convey controlled excitement. "Knock again to let us know you understand us."

There was a breathless wait, then another staccato rapping. Very nice. A breath of a chuckle sounded behind them, Giles simply irrepressible.

"Tell us what you want. Show us." Max was heaping coals on the fire. He was working them toward the cameo discussion like a steam train on the tracks.

Nothing happened.

Yes. Build them up. Then let them down. Like a penny dreadful novel. Every story had a rhythm. Disappointment now was essential to belief later.

Max's shoulders slumped. "Are you still with us? Please, let us know."

Still nothing, and Mrs. Calloway let out a disappointed sob. "Charlotte."

"Charlotte? Are you there?" Max called out as one would to a child, and this time the wind blew hard enough to make the candles stutter.

They needed new ones. He would talk to his friend Myron at the club. Surely his general goods store sold candles.

The wind whipped past them again, and the candles went out. A short scream came from the former nanny. "Something touched me!"

The candles lit once more, no one touching them. No one save Max, who was sweating now, his upper lip and hairline beaded with it.

Max needed to be careful. He needed to direct his energies efficiently. They would work on that.

"Charlotte! Answer us," Max demanded.

A positive flurry of knocking sounded through the room, as if squirrels or raccoons had invaded the upper floors and were wreaking havoc. He felt the sister on his right shaking, her hand sweaty, her grip desperate.

"Yes! Tell us, Charlotte. Tell us what you want!"

The figurine they had agreed upon shattered. At the same time, the wind seemed to swirl around them, and just as it had before, the cameo brooch appeared in the center of the table.

The first Andrew could attribute to Max.

The second had to be Charlotte herself.

He shook his head, his ears ringing, the smell of brimstone surprising him. His nose burned, his eyes watering.

Behind him, Giles cursed viciously, and jumped forward to tear his hand from the lady next to him. A lump of smoking sage landed in the middle of the table, covering the cameo, and Giles shouted something Andrew's remedial Latin had no name for.

They all blinked, and Max rose, moving to open the curtains.

Andrew glanced at Giles, who had lost all his smiles. He appeared fairly grim, in fact, his face pale and set in hard lines.

"Is everyone well?" Max asked.

"Shaken," said Mr. Calloway. "What the devil was that?"

To his credit, Max glanced at Giles, still playing the student to Giles' mentor.

Giles smiled, but the expression strained to hold on his face. "Can you ring for tea? I need to speak to you all very seriously and I think we could all use some sugar to help with the shock."

Calloway's bushy gray brows drew down. "Certainly."

"Excellent. Mrs. Calloway, will you come sit with me someplace comfortable?"

While Giles took the lady to the other end of the parlor, Andrew offered to help Max clean up.

"What on earth was that?" Max hissed as soon as the family had all moved to perch on parlor chairs and settees.

"Not a child, that's for sure. I suggest we see what Giles has to say and follow his lead."

Max grunted, but he didn't argue, so Andrew assumed they had settled on a plan.

Tea arrived only minutes later, and Giles waved for them to come sit.

"Now, Missus, you're not going to like what I have to say. You have to stop trying to contact the dead in this house."

Mrs. Calloway sniffed hard. "Why? My daughter is trying to communicate."

"No, ma'am. She's communicated. She wants the cameo that should have gone with her."

Mrs. Calloway went pale as milk, swaying.

"I told you, woman. I told you to let it go years ago. Charlotte was obsessed with that silly thing. Her great aunt brought it back from a grand tour of Italy."

"I couldn't." Tears streamed down her face. "I just couldn't get rid of it. It meant so much to her."

"Now you know." Giles took her hands in his. "If you keep trying to speak to her, you are inviting other, possibly evil spirits into your home."

"Evil?" Max raised his brows.

"Do you think something else tried to come in today?"

Giles nodded firmly. "I do. That smell… The burning. That was no benevolent spirit."

"What do we need to do?" Mr. Calloway asked.

"Bury the cameo." Max came out with that, looking to Giles, who smiled approvingly. "No more séances."

"Precisely."

Max nodded seriously. "I have never felt anything like we did today."

Mr. Calloway slowly straightened his shoulders. "We will bury it as soon as we can then. No, no arguments. This has become damned dangerous."

Mrs. Calloway dissolved into sobs, but Calloway would brook no argument. "Harriet, take care of her. Gentlemen, if you will come back to my study?"

They all rose, Max grabbing his bag while Andrew brought their tea cups. He'd put two sugars in each because he really thought they all needed something to calm their nerves.

Giles carried a plate of cookies as well as his cup, obviously having a similar thought. They settled in the study, all of them politely waiting for Mr. Calloway to begin.

He looked about. "Damn it all, I forgot my tea." He rang for a servant, who must have been on the way already, because she appeared with a cup of tea, leaving the room with a tiny bend of knees and chin.

"Now, then," Calloway said. "I want to thank all of you for your help." He glanced at Max. "I cannot have you back as I originally planned, however. It is not healthy for my wife."

"No, no, I would say not." Max glanced at Andrew, who raised a brow. "I'm so sorry if anything I did to try to help has caused problems."

"Nonsense. You allowed me to see that indulging this is causing her worse problems. It's time to put a stop to it."

"Perhaps," Giles said in a delicate tone, "you might think about steering her toward charitable activities. Orphanages."

"Mmm." Calloway tapped his fingers on the desk. "Yes, well. Who should I contact if we have problems after we bury the cameo?"

"Me. Max will be busy with clients." Andrew pulled out a card. It was the same one he'd given Max, with the club name and address. "Send a message there."

"Thank you." Calloway tucked it into his desk, then drew out an envelope to hand over to Max. "Your fee. I added a bonus."

"Thank you, sir." Max took it, managing not to look too eager, and they all sat for a moment, sipping tea and eating cookies.

Them, as one, the three of them on the non-business end of the desk rose. "Good day," Giles murmured.

"Good day, gentlemen."

Max clutched his bag, and Andrew and grabbed the bag Giles had brought. They walked out of the house, all of them drawing huge gulps of air.

"How stimulating," Giles said. "Back to the club, Andrew. I need to do some research."

"Yes, sir." He laughed, taking Max by the elbow. "Come with us."

"Oh, I—"

"Don't be silly, lad, Andrew wants to have sex with you. That's not to be missed."

"Giles!" Andrew tried hard not to laugh, because Max appeared near to keeling over from shock. "Really, it's one thing to say something like that aloud in the club. Here on the street it might get a man killed."

Max was gasping, mouth opening and closing like that of a landed fish.

"Really?" Giles blinked, back to the rather owlish persona he usually evinced. "Oh, do forgive me."

"Innocent does not look good on you, my friend." They reached the club in record time, and Giles waved at them in the lobby. "Come have supper with me in a few days, both of you. Such fun."

Then Giles disappeared through a hidden door, leaving Andrew shaking his head.

Andrew turned to Max, holding out a hand. "I really do want very badly to have sex with you right now, Max. Come upstairs with me?"

Max hesitated long enough that Andrew thought he would be rejected. Then one hand slid into his, and Max inclined his head. "I want you, too. Lead on."

Happiness bloomed deep and hot in his belly, and Andrew gripped Max's fingers, tugging him toward the stairs. Perhaps he would thank Giles for being so blunt after all.

Max's heart beat hard, his blood pumping fast through his veins. He held tight to Andrew's hand, following along to the second floor of the club.

If he were completely honest, Max was riding the high of

the incredible séance today, his whole self thrumming with energy. He could think of no better way to release it than to be with Andrew.

They ran suddenly, both of them laughing like schoolboys. Max felt wild, more free than he had since he was first on his own, before…

He couldn't think of his failures. Not now.

They stumbled into a private room, one with a bed draped with silk hangings. Andrew began divesting him of his clothes, and Max pried his other hand off the handle of his valise, dropping it to the floor.

He wrapped his arms around Andrew, begging a kiss, and receiving one that almost burned him to the ground.

Andrew moaned, moving him toward the bed.

Max broke away, gasping. "Your clothes."

"Shall I put on a show for you?" Andrew asked, hands on his jacket lapels.

"Please." Max's mouth was suddenly dry as dust, and he stared at Andrew, waiting, holding his breath.

Andrew slowly stripped off both coat and waistcoat, then tie and collar. He bent to remove his shoes and socks, and somehow that made Max sweat. Ridiculous, to be so aroused over bare feet, over a shirt open at the neck. He could see the swell of Andrew's cock against his fly, and he was proud that he had caused it.

Andrew paused, licking his lips and staring at Max. "Touch yourself for me, Max. I want to see how you need me."

His cheeks heated almost painfully, but Max complied, reaching for his cock with speed. He circled the base with his fingers before pumping up and down, his hips rocking. Surprising, how good his own touch felt at such a time.

"That's lovely. You're quite well-endowed, you know."

The compliment had him smiling, and if his cheeks got any hotter he would burn right up. He didn't know what to say, so Max spread his legs and showed off more, his balls swinging.

"Oh, Max." Andrew groaned the words. "I want such things."

"Do you?" He wanted to hear them. "Like what?"

"I want to spread you, taste your cock, put my mouth on you. I want to feel your greedy little hole on my tongue. I want to bind your cock and fuck you for hours, until you scream and beg for release."

His whole body jerked, and he had to grab his balls and yank them down to keep from spending. "The things you say."

Max had seen some engravings once, at a boarding house in New York City, where men had been fairly open about their relations. One in particular had made him sweat, made him touch himself late at night when he thought no one would know.

A man over the lap of another man, his ass exposed, the other man spanking him roundly as if he were a naughty child.

He wondered if Andrew wished to try that with him.

"What are you thinking about so hard?" Andrew undid the cuffs on his shirt, then the buttons down the front.

"Um." Max panted, stroking his cock. "An old engraving."

"Tell me about it?" Andrew tugged off the shirt, leaving Max with a view of a sportsman's chest, lean and well-muscled, no fat around the belly. Flat brown nipples tightened with exposure to the air.

"I— I admit, it excited me, but I fear it, too."

"Tell me," Andrew demanded. This time it wasn't a request, and Max found himself answering.

"A man. Being spanked by another man."

Andrew paused, hands on his waistband. Those bright blue eyes burned into him. "I vow, we must be made for each other, Max. Would you like to try it? I would spank your ass until it glows."

"Oh, good lord above." He had to pull his balls again, but a little spurt of fluid still dripped over the head of his cock and ran down the shaft. "Yes. No? I have no idea."

"I do." Andrew undid his buttons and slipped out of his trousers. "Get up on all fours, and I shall show you what it feels like."

"I— the engraving was of one man over the other's lap…" He wanted contact. Wanted that connection if he was going to do this.

"Was it indeed?" Andrew came to him, one hand sliding along his back. "Well, then. I don't want to disappoint you."

He knelt up when Andrew sat on the bed, uncertain.

Andrew knew what to do, pulling Max down so he lay across Andrew's thighs.

Feeling awkward and unbalanced, he pressed up with his hands, not wanting to burden Andrew with his weight.

"Shh." Andrew put a hand to the small of his back, pressing him down. "Just fold your arms under your head."

He did, because Andrew sounded so certain. He relaxed as much as possible. He breathed deeply, his cock rubbing Andrew's thigh.

"Now, I'm a bit rusty, so we'll start slow." Andrew caressed his ass with one hand, a soft touch that made the hair stand up on his neck.

"Andrew."

A stinging slap landed on his right buttock. "Hush. We do this my way, Max. Did today excite you?" Another blow, this to his left cheek. "Did it give you a feeling of power?"

"Yes!" His ass clenched, trying to shrink away from the explosive sting of Andrew's blows. They fell faster and faster, his skin burning with every slap.

Oh, God, the fire. The pain was humiliating but exhilarating. His cock felt harder than it had ever been, and Max arched, his will completely at the mercy of Andrew's touch.

He panted, rubbing, wiggling to get more friction on his dick.

"The more you fight, the more I spank, Max. You make me so hard. The way you wear the mark of my hand on your skin… God, I want you."

"Andrew." He panted out the one word, not able to say more.

A flurry of blows landed on the backs of his thighs, and Max's toes curled. He cried out at the unexpected feeling, his ass throbbing now in time with his heart.

"Please. Andrew, please."

"Be aware of what you're asking for, Max. I want to fuck you very badly."

"Yes." He had no idea what he was begging for, just that his skin was too tight, his body ready for the next level of pleasure.

"Very well, sweet." Andrew slid him back onto the bed and rose, moving to dig through a drawer in the bureau across the way. "Ah, perfect."

Andrew turned back to him, a small bottle in one hand.

"What is that?" Max had to kneel, because there was no way he could sit. None.

"Oil. We need it to ease the way."

"Oil." He repeated it rather stupidly. "Oh."

"Yes. Turn over on your back."

"But my—"

"I'll put a pillow under your lower back."

"So sweet." He gave Andrew a wry look, but eased down to his back, lifting up on his heels to allow Andrew to prop up his lower back. The position left his ass in the air, no pressure on it, but it also made him feel completely vulnerable. His cock bobbed up toward his belly, his balls swinging below.

"There now." Andrew stroked his inner thighs. "I'll get you ready."

"Yes." Max shuddered, his whole body on fire. He wanted whatever came next, wanted Andrew to possess him.

Andrew opened the vial of oil, the scent heavy but not spicy. He coated two fingers with it, and Max watched, his heart pounding against his ribs, while Andrew pressed those fingers between his legs. Sliding under his sac to find his hole.

Both fingers slid deep, Andrew pushing him to the very limit right from the beginning. Just as he had with the spanking, which made his ass burn and clench.

Max tried to breathe, tried to move, but Andrew place the other hand on his belly. "Shh. Bear down. Don't hold your breath. Push back with your hips."

"What does that mean?" Max burst out.

"It means relax, silly man." Andrew bent to kiss the tip of his cock, and suddenly Max did just that, his muscles loosening to allow Andrew in.

"Oh." He blinked, his nerves singing with the joy of it. "Scratchy."

"More oil, then." Andrew poured oil over his fingers where they met Max's ass. When he slid his fingers out, then back in, Max panted, nodding.

"Better," Max said.

"Perfect. Fuck, sweet. You're hot and tight inside." Andrew worked him open, an inch at a time, slowly but inexorably.

When he was panting, writhing, Andrew pulled free and knelt up close, the heat from his body like an inferno. Andrew slid into him a scant bit before pulling back, making Max want to yell at him to hurry, even if his body appreciated the care.

"Hold on and breathe, love." Andrew lifted Max's sore ass, shoving deep at last, a full-on attack on his senses.

He tried to breathe, but really, between the burning throbbing pleasure of his sore ass and the invasion Andrew was perpetrating, he had no breath left to hold. His world spun, lights dancing before his eyes.

He held onto something. Sheets maybe, or a coverlet. Max had no idea. His whole world had narrowed to his ass and that cock filling him.

His rear end stung and throbbed, the hairs on Andrew's legs burning his thighs.

He threw his head back and grunted when Andrew slammed deeper, the thrusts losing their slow rhythm.

Andrew chuckled, a breathless sound if admiration. "You inspire me, sweet."

"Good. Do it again." It wasn't a request.

Andrew's blue eyes narrowed, and he nodded before doing it again, the thrusts rocking him. He pushed back, meeting the thrust, slapping them together and making him gasp.

"Your skin is on fire. I need to blister your ass every time we fuck."

The things Andrew said made his toes curl right up.

"Tomorrow you'll remember me, with every motion, every second."

"I will." Max feared that, actually. What if he came to need this so badly he couldn't walk away? What if…

Another thrust rocked him, pegging lightning deep within him. He gasped, his eyes flying open wide, and Andrew met his shocked gaze, smiling.

"Feels good, doesn't it?"

All he could do was nod.

Nod and beg wordlessly for more.

Andrew gave him everything, anything he wanted. Max felt the impression of every one of Andrew's fingers, sinking in against his sore ass, holding him up. Every thrust rocked him, jolted him, built a fire in the pit of his belly.

Max panted, his body moving and rocking, trying to get closer. When Andrew lifted his hips even higher, he wrapped his thighs around Andrew's hips, keeping them connected.

"So much need, sweet. I ache for you."

"Yes. I—" He wanted to reach down and touch himself, but his hand didn't work.

Andrew pegged him, again and again, the sensations sparking flames deep within. His head hit the headboard, and Andrew yanked him back down so he was padded by the pillows. Max felt utterly owned, completely at Andrew's mercy.

"A man could lose himself in you, sweet."

"Yes. Please. Anything." He was babbling, and Max was very afraid things would start flying about any moment, but he couldn't stop now.

"If they do, we'll make a glorious noise."

He laughed, finally able to reach for his cock with one hand. "Oh, God."

"God has precious little to do with this."

"No. Not, this is pure devil." Even if Andrew did look heavenly, really.

"No. This is you and me. Us. Two men."

He met those sky colored eyes with his. Max nodded seriously, the moment lingering, stretching. "You and me."

"Indeed." Andrew leaned down and kissed him, the angle of the thrusts changing.

He put his free hand up, grasping Andrew's hair. The kiss pushed him to another place, another level of pleasure. His entire body tightened, his balls drawn close to his body. Max jerked at his cock, his muscles clamping down everywhere, holding Andrew tight, and Andrew cried out, the sound sharp, shocking.

He felt it when Andrew spent. Hot, wet seed spurted into him, and he clenched harder, holding it in. Andrew watched him, every second, the expression approving.

When Andrew reached between them, slapping his cock, Max shouted, his body trying to curl up as he shot, wet heat splashing in heavy ropes over his belly.

"Oh, sweet." Andrew slumped down on him, panting, laughing a little. That should have been insulting, but Max understood. The release of pressure inside him was enormous.

For the first time in his memory, he felt as if he could breathe.

Andrew kissed his throat. "Stay with me tonight, Max. I need you."

Max only nodded, stroking Andrew's sweaty back. Yes, he would stay. Tonight. After that, he had no idea what to do.

Chapter Seven

Andrew woke the next morning feeling as if he could take on the world. He and Max had spent the remainder of the day in bed, eating a decadent meal together, licking each other's fingers.

He stroked Max's back, watching his fingers slide over the fine skin. Max slept on his belly, and his ass still bore the imprint of Andrew's spanking. Delicious.

"I think I shall go and get something to break our fast. Would you like to come with me?"

Max just snuffled and buried his head under the pillow, so Andrew chuckled and rose, assuming his trousers. The wardrobe yielded a dressing gown and a pair of slippers, so he decided not to dress fully. None of his friends would care.

He stole another quick caress of that reddened ass, drinking in Max's low moan.

"I'll be back soon." He hummed, leaving the room and glancing at the hall. Goodness, someone was redecorating today. Left, then right.

The dining hall was bright and shining this morning, the sunlight pouring in from high windows. Ah, now, that meant the dining staff were in good moods. Excellent.

Andrew glanced about, always willing to stop and socialize for a moment. He saw Lionel sitting in the corner immediately under the windows, where no light would fall on him. Such a little dark cloud, his friend.

He smiled, lifting his hand in greeting before gathering himself some rashers of bacon, toast. He dipped out a bit of egg, then grabbed a pot of jam before joining Lionel.

"You look sour, Lionel."

"And you look like a ray of sunshine. Such happiness. It's disturbing."

"Nonsense. My lad and I have finished our current business and I enjoyed quite the night. I have no reason not to beam."

"Bah."

He chuckled. "That Horace lad move on?"

"They all do." Lionel waved a hand.

He reached for that hand and squeezed Lionel's fingers.

Lionel smiled faintly, but gripped his hand with surprising urgency. "All went well yesterday? No worries?"

"A few fits and starts, but nothing untoward."

"Good. Good. I worry about you messing with actual spirits. You're not meant for that."

"I brought Giles along with me, to facilitate."

"Ah. Excellent. Yes, Giles will have kept things at bay." Lionel released him. "I worry."

"It's good, to have a friend like you."

"Is it?"

Lionel's self-deprecating smile worried Andrew. His dear friend was in a truly odd mood.

"It is. You know I adore you. Do you need chocolate to improve your mood?"

"Perhaps. Perhaps that would lighten things for me."

"Let me get it for you." He went back to the breakfast array and found a pot of chocolate and a dainty cup and saucer. He hated to see Lionel in a black mood, scowling and off-balance. He would pick a variety of Lionel's favorites on a plate as well. By the time he returned, Lionel was smiling, the expression welcome.

"You're good to me."

"I am. You should be grateful."

"Eternally, you cad."

"Me?" He placed a hand over his heart. "I am the truest."

"Mmm. Fickle as the weather." Lionel was chuckling now, though, and Andrew smiled to hear it.

"I intend to offer Max a job today, to bring him into the fold, so to speak."

"Do you? Good for you." Lionel didn't seem ironic in the least. "I think he can do some fine work, if trained."

"He's done well without. I can only imagine his potential."

Lionel nodded sagely. "I can see what he means to you."

Andrew's cheeks heated. "It does seem meant to be."

"Excellent. You'll have to invite me to supper soon."

"I will. I promise." He ate his way through one plate, slapping Lionel's hand as he stole bites. They grinned and played, and he wanted Max to experience this camaraderie.

He suspected Max had been too many years in solitude, hiding his gift away. There were things deep inside Max that needed to be let out, secrets that no one man should have to take on himself. He remembered how bravely his Max had asked for his hand, for his cock, and his body tightened.

"Stop it." Lionel was laughing, eyes dancing. "Go on. Take a plate of treats back to your lazy lover."

He tried for innocent, but it was a lost cause. He'd lost any claims to innocence so long ago.

"Very well." He stood, then pressed a light kiss to Lionel's lips before moving to load up a plate of delicacies.

He looked back over his shoulder before he left, Lionel leaning back into the shadows.

Something about the dark slash of shadow falling over Lionel disturbed him, but Andrew knew Lionel could live with a great deal of darkness. He would be fine.

Besides, Max awaited him with that sweet, tanned ass. That was worth running back to their rooms immediately.

He put the tray down on the table, then went to the bed, to the man waiting there for him. Compact, athletic, Max was made for the kinds of games Andrew liked to play, and he shed his robe and trousers.

He leaned down, dragged his tongue over the still-heated skin of Max's ass, eliciting a low, near-desperate cry.

"Andrew? Oh, God."

"Yes, love." He chuckled, playing his fingers over the heated skin on Max's thighs. "Who else would it be?"

"This place is full of haunts." Max raised up to smile over one shoulder.

"No spirits would dare to touch you, not now."

"No? Why is that?" Max rolled over, then hissed.

"Because you're mine." Simple as that.

Max's eyes widened, his body stilling like that of a hunted animal. "What?"

"Shh." He ran one hand over Max's thigh, easing him. "They know you are under my protection, hmm?"

"Ah." Max nodded, relaxing. Then he grunted. "My ass is sore."

"Is it?" He traced the edge of Max's hip, right where the redness began.

Max twitched. "I haven't been so abused since my childhood."

"Mmm. I'll wager no one made you feel what I made you feel then."

"No. No, I can't say they did."

Andrew chuckled, sliding his hand under Max's balls to squeeze for a moment. Max's thighs popped open, the act as instinctive as breathing.

He nodded, then used his other hand to stroke the prick rising hard and hot from the nest of dark curls at Max's groin. The raw need made his mouth dry, made him shudder with pure desire. He could eat this man alive.

What a fine idea. He wondered how many times Max had experienced anything more than a hand on his cock. Andrew bent to close his lips around that prick he coveted so.

"Andrew!" Oh, what delicious shock.

He sucked hard, lips around just the head. Then he slid down, licking along the underside of the shaft. Max beat against the mattress, the sound wild and it made him smile.

Andrew licked and sucked, then pulled off to rub his stubbly chin against Max's cock.

"Fuck!" The little obscenity made him chuckle and repeat the gesture. Max was a well-educated, if destitute man. To see him devolve into the lowest common language excited Andrew unbearably. He reached down and tapped the sweet, swollen hole, waking those nerves up.

Max squirmed. "Please. I— sensitive."

"Mmm. Imagine if I had you hold it open and beat just your hole with a leather strap."

The low cry that filled the air was followed by a jerk of Max's heavy prick, a spurt of clear need falling to the flat belly.

"Yes. Confusing as it is enticing?" He licked Max's prick again, remembering how he'd taken all these same lessons at Lionel's hand. Andrew had proved far better at giving than receiving, but he knew just how Max felt. That odd mixture of arousal and vulnerability — for him it led to wanting to make another feel such a way, but he imagined Max would wallow in the sensations.

Max jerked up, trying to get him to take more, but Andrew pulled back, slapping Max's cock. "No. Greedy man."

Max gaped at him, lips parted, a look of pure shock on the handsome face. "Bastard."

"You have no idea, sweet." Andrew chuckled. "Shall I show you?"

Max nodded for him, eyes huge in his face. "Yes." The word came out slowly, as if Max could hardly believe he was saying it.

Andrew nodded. "Good, sweet. Good."

Had anyone ever needed so much? Ever? He doubted it. Andrew pondered what to do next. Maybe he should get the smaller leather strap, show Max what it felt like on his skin.

His mouth went dry at the options. Max was spread out before him, acquiescent, ready for his command.

He patted Max's leg. "Stay there. I'll be just over at the bureau. Right back."

Max nodded, eyes fastened onto him, following his every move.

He opened a drawer and found just what he was looking for. That happened a lot at Club Raven, often enough that he expected it, rather than be surprised by it.

He took up a small strap that was akin to a miniature razor strop, carrying it back to the bed. Andrew snapped it against his hand, then showed Max the mark on his palm.

Max's eyes went wide, the heat in them blazing. "Are you really going to—"

"Hands on the headboard, love, unless I need to bind you."

Max moaned hard. "No. I can hold on."

"Good. Good, sweet. Now grab hold."

Reaching up, Max held the headboard, muscles straining. The way he spread out, ready and trusting, honored him.

Andrew loved it.

"Beautiful." He ran one finger around the bone of Max's ankle.

"Th-thank you." Max's toes curled, and those eyes never wavered.

"Mmm." He touched the bottom of Max's foot, tickling the sole.

Max almost kicked him, but Andrew caught that foot before it connected with his ribs.

"Sorry."

"Sensitive," Andrew said, not worried at all.

"Yes. Yes."

Andrew adored the shock, the dazed confusion. Max was eager to learn, needing desperately, but a complete novice. As Giles would say, how diverting!

The first blow landed midway along Max's shaft, drawing a sharp gasp. Max arched up, his hands popping off the headboard to come down and cover his dick.

"No." Andrew strapped one hand. "Headboard. You said you did not require binding."

"Oh." Max's cheeks flushed, the pink tint spreading down his neck and chest. "No, I can be good." Max reached up again.

"I believe you can, if you try."

"I can." Max's chin jutted.

Andrew took that as the challenge it was, raising the strap so he could bring it down on the straining prick once more.

Max gritted his teeth, the lean hips punching up toward his blows. That red cock bounced and slapped at Max's belly before rebounding against the strap.

"Does it burn, sweet?"

"You know full well it does."

"I do. I've been where you are, Max. My Master had to tie me. I was far more suited to giving than taking."

Max wet his lips and held all the harder to the headboard. Muscles rippled in his chest and belly, and he swallowed hard. So pretty.

Andrew snapped the strap again, this time against the tip. Max's cry rang out, the sound spinning up into the ceiling. He gave Max a flurry of blows, working down to the base, dangerously close to the balls.

As he knew Max would, Max released the headboard, hands reaching for his wrists.

"No!" He snapped the word, and Max stopped dead, fingers clenching.

"Forgive me. I— That was so much."

"I understand, sweet." He did. Truly. "Back to the headboard."

Max's hands trembled as he reached up, wrapped them around the slats of the bed head.

"One more time and I will bind you, Max. Remember that." He slapped again, then again, varying the pressure and location.

"Yes." Max nodded and whimpered, throat working. "Stings. God."

"It does. It makes you feel alive, doesn't it, as if your skin is too small."

"Yes. Yes, exactly. Like my prick is huge."

"It's very nice." He wrapped the strap around the base, then rubbed it back and forth.

Max grunted, swallowing convulsively, hips rolling up toward his touch. He flicked the short end of the strap hard against Max's skin, then bent to blow on the stinging area.

"Please!"

Andrew was sure Max didn't know what he begged for. He did, and he uncurled the strap to rub it down over Max's balls and exposed hole.

The heavy sac drew up, wrinkling and tightening up toward Max's body. He was sure now that Max was almost afraid of what came next, so he backed off and snapped the leather against each nipple in turn. The tiny buds went tight and dark, drawing up to hard points.

Oh, now. Those had possibilities. Andrew set out to make them throb, make Max ache.

One slap after another, Andrew focused on making Max burn. Those tiny nubs of flesh swelled, grew almost purple. He would need clamps for them.

He leaned out, teeth fastening around out nip, and Max's hands landed in his hair, holding him tight.

Andrew let it go. Next time he would tie Max up and really let him understand vulnerability. This time he didn't want to chance Max breaking out his talent at the wrong moment.

"Please. Please, I burn. I burn."

"What do you want, sweet? You must ask." Every moment was a training moment, Lionel would tell him.

"I must spend. I need release."

"Not yet." Andrew wrapped the strap about Max's cock and balls. He didn't tie it but the loop would help ease things. They had more games to play this fine morning.

Many more.

He reached out to twist Max's nipples between his fingers, pulling them out away from Max's chest.

"Andrew!" Max sounded as if this was the most shocking

thing he'd done yet.

"Yes, sweet?"

"That hurts."

"Does it hurt, or does it feel good and you think it shouldn't?"

Max's cheeks went bright rose, the look pure shock.

"It's a natural reaction, Max." Andrew twisted again.

"Which part? What of this is natural?"

Andrew shook his head. "Never let anyone make you believe what we do is wrong." He cupped Max's jaw, stroked his lips with one thumb.

"You don't believe it's a sin?" Those gray eyes searched his face.

"Not a bit. You're willing, are you not?"

"I am." Max nodded firmly.

"As am I. No one is being forced here. There is no sin."

"Oh." Max appeared to consider that. "I— Kiss me?"

"Yes." That was an easy request to answer. Andrew leaned close and kissed Max's lips, the contact slow and sweet, Max opening up to him like a dream.

They kissed for a long time, deep and drugging, slowing things down, Andrew easing Max back into the sheets. He unlooped the strap from Max's privates and tossed it aside, knowing now they were only about each other.

Max drew him close, one hand hot and firm against his waist.

Andrew hummed and licked at Max's lips. So good. From heated to melted, this was all he could ask for.

He took Max's cock in hand, and Max stroked Andrew's, a closed circle. "Just so, Max. Just so."

Andrew bit that luscious lower lip and stroked faster, and suddenly they were on fire again, working hard. Panting, they rocked together, the heat rising in them like the blood in their cocks.

Max worked back and forth, rubbing Andrew's dick up and down. He was utterly focused, so beautiful it hurt. He dropped one kiss after another on Max's swollen lips, sipping the nectar from his lover's mouth.

Max pulled him even closer, getting their cocks together in one hand and jacking them, which would take them to the finish in no time.

"Clever lad," he teased, and Max winked at him, easy enough now to play.

They both lost words after that, their bodies rocking, sweat beading their skin. Andrew saw Max's eyes widen, knew he was about to go over, and leaned to kiss him one last time. They came together, hot seed falling between them, coating their skin.

The scent was pure perfection — the joining of both of them, rich and male and right. The musk floated up, and Andrew hummed happily before flopping down next to Max. "You amaze me."

"Me? Bah."

"It's true. I can't believe I found you."

"Neither can I." Max grinned over at him, so wicked.

Andrew reached out to stroke Max's cheek. "I shall have to keep you."

The look in Max's eyes went vulnerable, shy. "I have little to offer, Andrew."

"You have a great deal, so much that the club wants me to offer you a position, but that's business and this is not."

"Indeed." In that, Max seemed very sure. That suited him. They would talk business at breakfast.

"I brought you something to break your fast, Max."

"Did you?" Max slid up to sit, eyes lighting up.

Ah yes. He'd forgotten that his lover had missed more than one meal of late. He rolled off the bed to find the plate, the tempting delicacies still quite good. The fluttering touch to his ass made him gasp. He chuckled, turning back to Max with a smile on his face. "Eager."

"It was irresistible."

The urge to do a little dance almost overwhelmed him, but he sat instead, offering the plate.

"Did you eat? I can share with you."

"I did, but I will nibble. You were sleeping so soundly I didn't want to wake you, but I was peckish."

"You're generous with me. Thank you."

He sat cross-legged, reached for a tiny fruit tart. "You are my lover. It makes me happy to spoil you."

"I've never had a lover such as you, Andrew."

"I've never had one like you, either, Max. I want to teach you everything."

"Yes, please." Eager lad; it honored him, that enthusiasm.

"First you eat. Then we talk business." Andrew winked. "Then we can get back to pleasure."

"Business. I have to admit to a vast curiosity."

"Good. Now, eat your breakfast."

Max laughed and tossed toast at him, but then fell to eating like a ravenous man. They'd worked hard, after all. The rest could wait.

Max waited impatiently through breakfast, then through one interruption after another. As it happened, it was after noon before he and Andrew were able to sit down at luncheon and discuss this position he was being offered.

He wasn't sure exactly what a gentleman's club might need with someone of his gifts, but he was more than willing to hear Andrew out. In fact, he was eager to discover what terms the club could offer. He was tired of living hand to mouth, but even more, he wanted to be near Andrew.

Andrew smiled for him when they settled at a table in the dining room, appearing a bit harried. "Really, love, I had no idea so many people would need us."

"You are a popular man; I can see that."

"I'm usually here for a few hours and then I leave. That I stayed overnight is news." Andrew shook out his napkin. "They say it's chicken pie for lunch today."

"Excellent." Honestly, what was the damnable job?

Andrew put his elbows on the table, a rather shocking move for such an educated, polite man. "Now, then, the position. Many of us work for the club. In fact, I was acting on their interests when I came to your first séance."

"They wanted me stopped? I was hurting no one."

"No, they wanted to see if you were a fraud or the real thing." Andrew shrugged. "That's my job."

"And what will mine be?" He didn't know many people like him, frauds or no.

"I imagine there will be any number of things. You have the potential to have very fine control. There are things, energies, that someone of only your talent can mend."

He had no idea what he could mend, what he could do, but he allowed that Andrew knew more about this than he did.

Andrew chuckled. "One of the other members would be able to help more. I know my talent, and I can sense what others can do, but helping you hone it would not be my strong suit. I'll get us a meeting with Julian."

"So why do they want me? Surely they have men already."

"Because we're waging something of a war, love." Andrew frowned as if searching for words. "The club is… alive, Max. It needs balance."

Andrew had lost his mind. That was the only explanation.

"Lads!" Giles, the archivist he'd met at the séance, plopped down at the table with them. "There you are."

Lord, the little man was…pure bouncy energy.

"Giles. Did our discussion call to you?"

"It did. How did you guess?"

"Because you're nosy." Andrew winked. "Charles, another place setting, please."

"Of course, Master Andrew. Immediately."

"Thank you." Giles beamed. "Did I hear that our ghost moved on?"

Andrew nodded. "We believe so."

"Most excellent!" Giles glanced at him. "Did he offer you the job?"

"He did."

"But he could hardly explain it." Giles chuckled. "We've been tasked with containing a force far bigger than any one of us, Max. You have seen the spiritual force of one ghost now, yes?"

"Yes. Yes, she was totally real." No question whatsoever.

"Precisely. Now imagine a place where many, many forces such as that converge. A place that draws them."

"You think I can get rid of them, too?"

"I think you have skills that will work well on certain energies, yes. That's all you do, you see. Manipulate energy to lift things."

Lift things. He did that, he supposed. Moved them. Threw them, more often.

Periodically he just toppled them over.

He grinned a little. "Well, if you folks want to pay me to do whatever, I suppose I need to ask how much?"

"Straight to the point, direct." Giles bounced in his chair. "I like it."

Andrew nodded at him. Andrew and Giles shared a glance. "Twenty dollars a week, plus room and board to begin."

Max blinked. The average wage for a decent working man was ten dollars a week, tops. "Plus room and board? Here?"

"Yes." Giles smiled. "Once you're on your feet you may decide to rent lodging elsewhere, but the club has many rooms."

"Yes." He didn't bother to negotiate. He needed the work and, more than that, he needed to be near Andrew. He could go to Mrs. Casey's boarding house and get his things and never return.

"Good." Giles held out a hand to shake.

He took Giles' hand and gasped, a burning sensation piercing his palm. Max stared at his hand when he drew back, expecting to see a mark.

Giles just appeared so pleased.

Andrew stared at him, blue eyes burning with bright emotion, with heat for him.

"Giles. We have an appointment." Andrew's voice was nearly a growl.

"We do?" Giles stared back and forth between them. "Oh, you mean with each other? I see. I shall go and sit with Joseph and Samuel."

"Thank you, Giles." Andrew stood, almost dragging him up. "We'll have our food delivered to our room."

Max licked his lips. "Yes. Please."

Charles the waiter came to clear away their drinks. "Very good, sirs."

"Now, Max. Now."

He ducked the easy swat, his backside still aching. He ran out of the room, but got confused when he entered the hall. Which way?

He turned back to the dining room, shocked to find a blank wall. "Andrew?"

"Come along, sweet." Andrew caught his hand from the wrong side, he thought, tugging him along.

"The walls…"

"Not now, sweet." Andrew towed him like a yearling colt, never letting him slow until they reached the room they were staying in.

For whatever reason, Andrew was lit up, slamming him back against the door and taking a wild kiss.

He wrapped his arms around Andrew's neck, his whole lower body on fire. His ass and his cock were lit up from the beatings, and he found himself thrusting wildly, driving madly against Andrew's strength.

Andrew groaned, pushing him faster and faster, hands dragging at his clothing, stripping him down. His cock was taken in one hard hand, the fingers squeezing tight.

The burn took his breath, the sweat and pressure making his skin flame, it seemed. Max cried out, breathless and unable to control his body.

"Let it go, Max. Let the energy go."

"What? What are you—" He gasped, his balls drawing up as he shot, his seed falling over their skin like heavy raindrops.

"Good. Good man. Now me."

Dazed, he reached for Andrew's cock, fumbling, but finding it hard and wet at the tip. It wouldn't take long, just a stroke or two. He squeezed, tugging, working his hand up over the head.

"Good. Again, sweet. Again."

"Like this?" He tugged and pinched a tiny bit.

"Yes!" Andrew went up on tiptoe, pushed into his touch.

"I can do that." He could do more. Max was willing to give what Andrew needed.

He'd never seen someone so free, so wild in pleasure. Andrew was— well, Max had never known anything like Andrew, who was a force of nature. Addiction.

He wanted to learn everything — everything about his new lover. Max had no idea how long this could possibly last. Luck wasn't his strong suit. So he had to take what he could and run with it.

Andrew's lips crashed against his, tongue pressing in, mimicking the acts of last night.

He tightened his grip on Andrew's prick, wanting to feel Andrew spill. Now. He wanted the ultimate proof of Andrew's desire.

And he got it. Andrew cried out, the sound almost a song, and rocked into his fist, spending for him forcefully.

His spent cock throbbed, losing a spurt of seed. Max rubbed the come into their skin, his knees sagging.

Andrew caught him, waltzing him to the bed where they flopped down. "Better. Much better."

"What was that? Out in the hall?" The rooms had... moved. Changed order.

"Hmm?" Andrew looked more curious than deceptive.

"The door to the dining room was gone when we turned around."

"Smoke and mirrors. It will stop once you are regular, for the most part."

"Andrew." He blinked. "Walls do not move."

"The club is kinda alive." Andrew chuckled.

He wasn't sure that was plausible, but then again, he'd seen a ghost. Who knew what went on in these… what had Andrew called it? Convergences?

"You're thinking very hard for a man who has just climaxed."

"Am I?" Max laughed. "Maybe you need to work harder."

One of Andrew's eyebrows climbed up into his hairline. "Is that a challenge, my boy?"

His cheeks heated almost painfully, but he wasn't above wanting more of Andrew's unique lovemaking. "Yes."

"Oh, you are a treasure, aren't you?"

"I hope so." He spread out on the bed, pushing up on his heels to offer his body.

"Look at you. What fun we will have."

"Can we start now?" Max asked, winking when Andrew laughed. Soon enough he would have to start this new job and go close his old one down. Right now he just wanted to play.

Chapter Eight

Andrew woke to the sound of Max's belly growling. Gracious, breakfast had been a long while ago. He rubbed his own belly, then scratched a little simply because it felt good.

He had a compatriot, a lover, someone to educate in the peculiar games they played together. Oh, he knew Max would have to spend time with a mentor for his talent, too, but Giles would decide who that mentor would be.

Sneaky bastard had his fingers in all the pies.

The corner of the blanket lifted of its own accord, baring Max's foot.

He shot a glance at Max's face, but his lover was sound asleep. Curious.

Max curled his leg, hiding his foot under the coverlet again. As soon as he did, the blanket was tugged away again, leaving both feet bare.

Andrew raised his eyebrows. He felt no talent being used. None. How odd.

"Are you playing with us?"

Perhaps one of the club spirits were having fun with them.

The blanket fluttered. Ah, so someone was in here, teasing them. "Really, we're fine on our own, please."

"Who are you talking to, then?" Max sat up and stretched, his back popping.

"No one, I suppose." He would speak to Giles. Maybe to his friend, Samuel, who saw ghosts.

"Mmm. Someone might think you were quite mad."

"Would they?" He was chagrined, honestly. He prided himself of discerning talents, and he thought perhaps he had Max's all wrong.

"I tease. No one believes ill of you, I'm sure."

"Oh, I'm sure many people do. Not here, though. We may not all be friends, but we're in the same boat." Although he had to wonder if perhaps he'd mistaken whether Max paddled a canoe or a rowboat.

"You look angry." Max yawned again. "How can you be mad after the night we had?"

Was he angry? He was frustrated, perhaps, concerned. He wasn't angry at all.

Andrew slid a hand over Max's bare ankle. "I'm not mad at all. In any way."

"Good. I would hate to have soured you already."

"Nonsense!" He slid back down next to Max. "I am often accused of thinking too much."

Max reached for him, stroked his belly gently. Soothing him.

He smiled. "I was thinking about ghosts, actually." There. That would keep Max from worrying he was the cause of ill humor.

"Ah. Yes, that was unusual, wasn't it? A real ghost finding me?"

"Mmm." He wondered how many might be tagging along.

Max drew random patterns along his chest, teasing him, playing idly.

"Your stomach was growling."

Max's cheeks heated, and he shrugged. "I hope I didn't wake you."

"No, love. Stop being so worried."

"It's my natural state, I'm afraid."

"Is it?" He petted in return, stroking Max's hip. "Why?"

Max shook his head, cheeks going a deep rose.

"You can tell me, sweet."

"I have bad luck," Max blurted.

"Pardon me?" What utter nonsense.

"I do! The only thing I had approximating a lover before you got bashed in the head with a falling barn rake the first time we tried to… you know. There have been many things like that. And then in Philadelphia…" Max went pale, shaking his head.

"Love?" He reached out, hand dragging along Max's back.

"There was a fire," Max whispered. "I was doing a séance. I lost control and flames hit the drapery. No one was hurt, but the family lost everything." Max's agonized whisper tore at Andrew's heart.

"Oh, my dear." Fire could be a brutal thing. They'd had a few firebugs in the Raven and, honestly, they hadn't been able to stay.

"I don't know what happened. I just don't." Those gray eyes looked so haunted.

"Well, accidents do happen." And that tickle in the back of his mind became an itch.

"But I had never had such a lack of control. It was almost…"

He waited, then pushed, just a bit. "Almost?"

"Well, today. Yesterday?" Max laughed, sounding strained. "Whatever day it was we were at the Calloways. It was so similar."

"How so? In circumstance?" He kept touching — partially to allow Max not to feel alone, but mainly because he needed the connection.

"As if it wasn't me. I just assumed it was, but what if it was a real spirit?"

"Ah, I can see where that would be disconcerting. Did you sense an anger? An emotion?"

"No. I mean, it was the physical sensations. The cold, the wind." Gooseflesh covered Max's arms and he drew the man closer.

"I wonder if it wasn't a spirit, Max. Perhaps you've had more than you know."

"Surely I would have known; one would have made itself clear to me?"

"I would think so, but sometimes it's not that easy." He

wanted to speak to Giles, to see if there were personal ghosts hanging around Max. If there were, that put things in a whole new light.

Not a better light, but new.

Max shrugged, clearly uneasy. "I hope it's just coincidence."

"Well, if you'd like, we can arrange a discussion with Giles."

"I'm willing." Max grabbed and held his hand. "Later?"

"Much," he agreed.

"Thank you." Max settled against him. "Do you think it's too late for food?"

"Here? Never. The kitchen is rather preternatural."

Max raised an eyebrow. "I think I'm afraid to ask if you mean it."

Andrew chuckled. He felt once Max learned about the ins and outs of the club, he would never worry about whether something was natural or not.

"You can laugh, but it's all new to me." Max squeezed his hand.

"That's part of the point, isn't it? That it's all fresh for you?"

"I suppose so." Max suddenly looked terribly young and uncertain. "I hope you don't bore easily."

He answered by reaching out and cupping Max's still-heated backside.

Max jumped, then laughed softly. "I know that I won't tire of that."

"You don't think so?" Andrew tapped his ass.

"No. I mean, I find it very stimulating."

He chuckled under his breath and patted again, and again, harder each time.

Max wiggled, his breath coming faster.

"Needy little wanton. Begging for more."

"I— yes. Yes, I am."

"Mmm. Over my knee again, lad. I foresee this being a daily thing."

"Daily?" Max did crawl right into his arms, allowing him to bend Max over his lap.

"Don't you think so? A bit of warming?"

"Warming." Max made a wondering sound. "Not punishment?"

"Not in the least. A connection, a heat, a passion."

"Oh." Max settled, asscheeks pink already.

This was slow and easy, just a steady rain of blows that were meant to arouse and heat, nothing more. Andrew's hand tingled from it and he could only imagine how Max's sweet backside would feel.

Those thighs spread wide, a hint of the tiny wrinkled hole appearing, the heavy balls. Oh, lovely. What a sweet sight.

He tapped that entrance with two fingers, knowing Max would feel the strapping.

"Dear Lord." Max gasped and twisted, trying to move closer and away all at once.

"Yes. You see, sweet. Pleasure."

"Please. Yes. Yes, I see."

He tapped a few more times before whacking that warmed ass harder, really letting Max feel it. Andrew wanted them to bond well over this. He needed his Max to understand that this — this wonder was theirs.

This was about them together. Not because Max was acting out or needing correction, although they might learn to play those games, too. This was about skin on skin.

"I have need of you, Andrew!" The cry was soft, but aching with hunger.

"And I you, sweet. I want everything you have to give me."

"Everything. Please!" Max wriggled off his lap, the reddened arse held carefully aloft, lips wrapping around his cock like a heated sleeve.

Andrew shouted, one hand gripping Max's hair, his hips rising and falling. He bounced upon the mattress like a madman, driving up and up into Max's lips. So utterly unexpected, this hard loving Max applied, giving him no quarter, expecting him to fight for his control — both over Max and over himself.

Andrew took on the task, gritting his teeth so he might slow his motions, his muscles screaming at him.

Max whimpered, the suction going hard and fast.

"Shh." He tugged Max off his cock. "Not yet, sweet."

Max stared up at him, lips swollen, eyes huge. He read the need there, the utter confusion.

"I want inside you."

Max moaned, reddened ass lifting higher in the air.

"Yes. You know where the oil is, sweet."

And he wanted Max to participate in his own fucking.

"Yes. I know what to do now." Max reached for the oil. Then he knelt up so Andrew saw him pour oil over his fingers.

Andrew's mouth went dry as dust, and he swallowed back his cry that begged to be released. His cock ached to be where Max was touching, where those fingers disappeared, then reappeared. Soon, he told himself. Soon it would be his.

He reached to tug down his balls, because he needed to hold on. Andrew was not going to give up the chance to feel Max around him again.

How quickly his sweet wanton learned these lessons. Andrew was so damned proud.

How many times did he find a boy, then lose him to hysteria and drama? Not that way for Max. He needed these touches, their games.

Max, perhaps, needed him.

Andrew knew he could fast become addicted to this one. He would have to hang on to Max. He grunted when Max poured oil on his cock. Now a good, hard fuck.

"Hands and knees, boy. I need to see your ass, all red for me."

Max paused, then shuddered with obvious pleasure. He scrambled up to hands and knees, presenting his flushed bottom.

"Luscious." He traced a lazy circle with his finger, letting his nail drag.

Max curled up like a cat being stroked. "I'm ready."

"You most certainly are." He wasted no time and gave no quarter, pressing in to spread Max wide.

"Uhn." Max's soft grunt sent shivers up his spine.

Oh, that noise was lovely and one he wanted to hear again. He thrust in again, deep as he could on one go.

"Andrew!" Not a grunt, but perfectly acceptable.

"Yes. Fast now, sweet. I feel like a hard ride." He didn't wait for a response. Instead, he claimed what he craved. He spanked Max again, this time with his hips, and it earned him a gratifyingly loud cry.

"Andrew, I vow!"

"What? What will you give me, Max?"

"All I have, I swear to you. All I am."

"That's a fine start." He bared his teeth, gripping Max's hips and slamming forward. "I accept."

The words rang with magic, with intent.

Max clamped down around him, muscles rippling, squeezing him. He gritted his teeth, driving in faster, harder, slamming them together.

"More. Please. Andrew. I need it." Max babbled, slapping back against him.

"Demanding boy." He swatted Max's well-spanked ass, making it sting.

"Oh!" Max arched up, almost crawling away.

"No." He snagged Max's hip, tugging him back.

"I can't."

He slapped again, keeping Max against him with the other hand. "You can, and you will. I need you here."

"Yes." Max nodded, hair flying violently.

"Exceptional answer." He swatted once more, and Max's ass rippled around his cock.

"Only answer." Max panted the words out, body rocking back and forth.

"Yes." His entire body shuddered, his hips pressing deep as his balls drew up.

"I want to feel you spend in me."

Wicked man. Lovely, wicked man. Andrew had to bite him, had to lean over that steaming ass and nip at one shoulder, allow his teeth to sink in and leave a mark.

Max shouted, right muscles closing around him so hard he couldn't breathe, his cock squeezed so tight he had to yell. Andrew shot his seed deep into Max, his little death impossible to ignore. He filled his lover up with his heat, staying buried deep.

Then he reached down and grabbed Max's swollen cock, jerking it hard and fast. He felt every touch, every tug, all around his need.

Max thrust into his hand several times before hot jets of seed issued from him, coating the top sheet. Oh, the scent was divinely earthy.

He was quickly becoming a genuine fool for his man.

Max flopped down on the bed, then began to laugh, a joyful sound which surprised the hell out of him.

"What's so funny, Max?"

"I am. Spanking me like a naughty child, and I love it. I crave it, Andrew." Max sobered. "Am I a deviant?"

"Don't be ridiculous. What men of our cut crave may be outside the norm, but that is all. I have needs that you fill; it is only right that I do the same for you."

"I—" When Andrew's cock slipped free, Max turned to face him. "You sound so sure."

"I am." Andrew refused to seem otherwise. This was his home, his world, his life's work and he would not doubt it.

Max slipped a hand into his. "At some point I need to go retrieve my things."

"Shall I assist you?" He admitted to a curiosity about all things involving Max.

Max frowned, his cheeks going red. "No. No, I have very little, and I have my work items here in my bag. Just some clothes and a few books."

He reached up, touched one hot cheek, and frowned. "Are you sure?"

"I had to stay at a rather dubious accommodation."

Andrew shook his head. "You have nothing to be ashamed of, Max. Nothing. I was a soldier. I have sleep in rat infested hospitals. I have no wish to embarrass you, but I am happy to help."

He had been forced into squalor as a soldier, and God knew he had sought it out more than once, before Lionel had brought him to the club. In fact, Lionel had found him in an opium den, trying to escape the buzz in his head as he rode the serpent.

"I want you to know me as I am, Andrew. Right now."

"Then you take your heated little ass out today to get your things and come back to me and never look back." Andrew tugged Max to him for a kiss. In time Max would trust him with every secret, but for now, he would allow this little privacy.

Max nodded. "Would you bathe with me? I saw a rainbath! I've never used one."

"Indeed." He loved the happy excitement in Max's eyes. Andrew rose, tugging Max with him. He loved the rainbath, the stinging little drops of water that felt natural, but were warmed by the furnace to a heated pleasure.

It was the height of decadence, and, if he were fortunate, he might get yet another rise from his eager lad.

He grinned. That was worth delaying Max's trip back to his boarding house, wasn't it?

Andrew thought so, for certain. In fact, he decided he would do whatever it took for such an event to occur.

Max hurried into Mrs. Casey's boarding house, hoping the lady herself was readily available. He was paid in full for the week, but he wanted to leave her in a good frame of mind should he need to return, so he wanted to give her an extra dime as a cleaning fee.

He was employed now; he could afford such luxury.

Mrs. Casey was busily giving orders to the staff, such as they were, pointing here and barking commands there.

"Mrs. Casey? May I have a moment?"

She looked up at him, as if sizing him up, then nodded once. "Everyone out."

People scattered like mice in the presence of a large cat.

Max had to admit, it was impressive and his balls drew up in pure self-defense.

She bared her teeth. "Well? What is it, Max?"

"I've found other accommodations, permanent ones, so I'd like to offer you a cleaning fee, ma'am."

"Would you now?" She put her hands on her ample hips, then threw her head back to laugh. "You've always been too fine for my place, lad."

"I have a position near the harbor. Good work." Honest work, or so he hoped.

"Good, good. No need to pay me more. I'll use your week's rent to clean. If you should need me, well, you come back."

Max allowed himself to smile at her. She was a force of nature. "Thank you, Mrs. Casey. I'll go collect my things."

"Best of luck to you, lad."

"Thank you, Missus." He waited for her to nod before he left the room, making his way upstairs to his room. He checked between the ticking and ropes of the bed to make sure he'd left nothing behind before gathering his clothing.

"Where are you going?" The words shocked him and he stood too fast, his aching arse reminding him of the pleasures he'd enjoyed.

He whirled about to look at the young man standing in the doorway. Max couldn't remember seeing him before. He would remember, because the man was striking, lean and not tall in stature, with a shock of rich, black hair streaked with pure white. He also bore mismatched eyes, one green, one blue.

"I-Home. I'm heading home. I'm sure the missus will rent

you my room."

"Your room does seem bigger than mine." The man wandered inside, sliding one almost delicate hand over the dresser's edge.

"Not mine anymore." His heart began to trip hammer in his chest.

"I suppose so. You're going where the ravens are."

He blinked, his mouth going dry. "Pardon me?"

"You are." The smile the man gave him lit the whole room. Astonishing. "I'm Vincent. I have to warn you, Max. I must. Something followed you and your love home. Something wicked." The look in Vincent's eyes was not a bit mocking, not mocking, but worried. "You must take care, because it will wear a mask."

"What do you mean?" This man… Andrew would say he had a talent. A gift. To Max, Vincent appeared cursed.

"I wish I knew. I'm sorry. I only know what I know."

Max repeated the words to himself so he could tell Andrew. Then he took an impulsive step forward to grasp Vincent's hand. "If you ever need me, come to Club Raven on Cathedral Street."

"Yes?"

"I swear. Ask for Max. They will find me."

Vincent gifted him with another of those amazing smiles. "Thank you. I will."

He stood there, dazed for a moment, then when he blinked again, Vincent was gone. Vanished.

Had he been a ghost? Max's hand tingled from a very real touch and when he lifted his fingers, they smelled of pomade.

So very much alive.

He gathered the last of his things and left the rented room without a backward glance. One of the ladies of the night he knew in passing waved to him from her doorway, and then he was out and on his way back to Andrew.

He had a paltry few things on his journey home, and he hurried, repeating Vincent's words to tell Andrew. Max didn't want to forget. It seemed too important.

He slowed as he reached the carved front doors of the Club Raven, suddenly convinced that he would be turned away. His nerves jittered, and he stopped on the stoop, shifting from foot to foot.

Just as he raised his hand to knock, the front door opened. "Why are you standing out here, Master Max?"

"I was just arriving." That was a fair enough answer, wasn't it? Especially since he had no idea who this fellow was or how the man knew his name.

"Master Andrew is waiting for you in the dining room. Upstairs."

"Yes, sir. Thank you. I... I don't suppose you might lead the way?"

"I fear I am on door duty. However, Daniel will meet you at the second floor landing to lead you from there." The fellow gave him a cheerful smile and padded off to some unknown post where he could no doubt spring out at unsuspecting guests.

Right. Up the stairs and look for...did he know Daniel?

He made his way to the grand stairs and trotted up to a man who stood staring out of blank, blind eyes. "Master Max?"

"Yes. Master Andrew is waiting for me in the upstairs dining room?" He hated how unsure he sounded.

"Indeed, sir. He is at a sitting with Mister Lionel and Joseph and Samuel. This way, please. I am Daniel."

"Ah. Daniel. Pleased. The doorman told me to search you out."

"His name is Zane." Daniel paced steadily ahead of him, delivering him to the room he'd been to so many times, but by a route he'd never seen before.

"Zane." He repeated the name silently. One of the most important things in life was to remember the people that served you. If you were good to them, they would be good to you.

"Yes, sir. He's angling to become Mister Lionel's next young man."

Lionel — Andrew's dear friend. "Excellent."

If Lionel was developing another tete-a-tete then the man would leave Andrew alone. Max immediately felt a stab of guilt for thinking it, but he knew they had been lovers, and Max wanted that role for Andrew now.

More than now, he thought. Forever.

The dining room was nearly deserted, which made him wonder what the hell time of day it was. Inside the club, time seemed as fluid as the order of the rooms. Days came and went at their own rate, and the world inside spun.

He smiled when Andrew saw him and rose, holding out a hand.

Daniel detained him for a moment, hand on his valise handle. "Shall I take this to your room?"

He'd forgotten his things altogether. How unlike him.

"Please, if you don't mind." He was never going to be better than the gauche charlatan that caused damage wherever he went. He wanted to slink away, but Andrew waited.

"Yes, sir." Daniel took his bag away and Andrew came to meet him.

"All packed and moved, then?" Andrew asked, taking his hand to lead him back to their lunch.

He nodded, offered a wan smile to the table. "All done."

"Excellent. Is something amiss?" Andrew turned him, facing him once more.

"Someone at the boarding house gave me a warning, a rather dire one." Max said it before he thought, but Andrew had told him more than once that he could speak freely among the members.

"Oh, I do love a dire warning." That was from a dapper, dark-haired man sitting next to Lionel. "Come tell us."

"He said that something followed us home. Something hidden enough that we ought to take care." Max shifted from foot to foot, giving the dark man a strained smile.

Andrew sat, tugging him down into a chair that sat very close. "Really? Who was this?"

"Vincent." He shrugged, knowing that his answer was less than satisfying.

Lionel leaned his elbows on the table, a deliberately rude gesture. "Who is Vincent?"

"One of the lodgers. I think you should meet him," Max told Andrew. "You would be intrigued."

"Is he a close friend of yours?" Andrew asked.

"I'd never met him before today."

Andrew shared a glance with the other men at the table. "Then you shall have to show me your old abode anyway. I will want to meet him. Did he say anything else?"

"That the wickedness wore a mask."

"I see." Lionel drawled the words, making everyone else glance at him in surprise. "What utter nonsense."

Max felt his cheeks heat, and he forced himself to breathe, to keep his visage still and quiet. Lionel clearly thought he wasn't good enough for Andrew, but Max intended to prove him wrong, starting now. He, at least, would mind his manners.

"No." The man who hadn't spoken yet said it, his voice sounding as if he was gargling stones.

Lionel shot the man a scathing look, but surely he couldn't see it with those pure black eyes.

"Max, this is Joseph and his boy, Samuel."

Max started, staring back and forth between them. His boy? What did that mean? Samuel was of age, and from his scars, Max thought he had experienced a good bit of the world, as well.

"Pleased to meet you." Manners. Above all else, manners.

"Pleasure is all ours." The dapper little man held out a hand and shook his when he offered. Samuel didn't touch him, but he got a nod, a hint of a smile.

"Really, do you always listen to strangers at a boarding house?" Lionel asked with a sneer.

"Lionel!" Andrew snapped out. "Do I need to send you to your room?"

"Pardon me?" Lionel actually bared his teeth and a frisson of worry buzzed along the nape of Max's neck. He didn't know the man well, but something about the way Lionel's face changed arrested his attention.

Andrew seemed more annoyed than concerned. "You're acting an ass. Be good, will you? You've been a regular bear with a sore paw of late."

"Perhaps I have. Perhaps I need a willing man over my knee." Lionel gave Andrew a look that put Max's back up, sultry and lustful.

"Daniel tells me Zane downstairs is willing." Max said it before he could stop himself, the words popping out in an insolent tone.

"Max!" Andrew's voice was a mixture of amusement and shock.

Samuel chuckled, a raw, painful sound that nonetheless made Max smile. "True enough. Zane's new, but he's damned eager, and I have seen him cast his eyes on Lionel more than once."

"Perhaps I'll go down and renew our acquaintance. It's preferable to the nonsense here." Lionel rose, a lean, beautiful man with an ugly expression his face. It seemed so odd. When Lionel sailed out of the room, nose in the air, Joseph turned to Andrew.

"What on earth is wrong with him?" Joseph asked.

"Max is moving in," Andrew said, placing a hand over his. "Perhaps he's a bit put out."

"Oh." There was a wealth of meaning in that single word.

He turned his hand beneath Andrew's, twining their fingers together. He rubbed at Andrew's hand with his thumb, feeling proud that Andrew was not denying him, was pleased to be with him.

"Well, now, Lionel knew better than to think y'all could be together long," Samuel said. "He'll get over it." There was a long pause, a wicked grin. "Or not. Either way."

"Welcome to Club Raven, Max," Joseph said. "I understand

you've accepted a position here."

"I have." Anticipation curled in his belly. "I can't wait to explore what I can do for the club."

"My boy and I also are employed here." Joseph reached out, hand petting Samuel's long hair.

"Really?" His interest piqued, Max leaned forward, hands on his knees. "What do you do?"

"Samuel can see phantasms, whether or not they wish to be seen."

Samuel nodded, jet eyes on him. "They cover you like a cloak."

Max jerked back, looking about him wildly. No, he didn't carry spirits with him. He'd never seen one until little Charlotte. "What?"

"You got to know. There's many."

"Samuel." Joseph's voice was low, gentle. The command was there, nonetheless.

Those black as night eyes turned to Joseph for a long moment before Samuel nodded, sitting back in his seat.

Andrew sighed. "I thought as much. After the last séance..."

"Thought what?" What? Were they talking about him? Gossiping? What ghosts? He hadn't even believed in them until the disaster at the Calloway house.

"When we did the last séance I wondered, sweet. I had planned to speak to Samuel once you settled in." Andrew stared steadily at him, no signs of dissembling present.

"So what do they want?" He sat very still, his hands flat on the table.

"I reckon they're feeding on you. You use them; they use you."

He blinked at Samuel. "Feeding?" He swallowed hard. That sounded awful. He wanted to throw up.

"Master?" Samuel looked to Joseph.

"They use your energy and you use theirs."

Master? Was Samuel a servant? Max shook his head. He didn't understand any of this.

"I'll explain it all, Max. You have nothing to fear. I think they've been with you a long time." Andrew took his hand again, and he felt better immediately, the nausea fading.

"Forgive me. Everything seems new—the world is suddenly changed." Max stood, not wishing to be rude, but he simply couldn't sit still another second. The idea that spirits surrounded him chilled him to the bone.

"Of course." Joseph gave him an easy smile, and Samuel nodded.

Andrew, on the other hand, tugged him back down by his captive hand. Right onto Andrew's lap.

"Andrew!" Oh, he did fit there and, he had to admit, that sudden pressure twinged certain tender parts deliciously.

"What? We're among friends. I promise you will find that true." Andrew pinched his asscheek.

"Indeed. This is not a place to pass judgment, is it, boy?" Joseph fed Samuel a tiny treat.

"No, Master." Samuel's expression lightened to something transcendent when he looked at Joseph. Something joyful.

It was almost painful to watch—so intimate, so private. He wanted that with Andrew, although he didn't see why Samuel called Joseph master.

"I will explain everything in time, Max. You have my oath." Andrew hugged him gently.

Max nodded, because he wanted to believe. Then he did the unthinkable and lifted his face, begging a kiss.

"Very nice." Andrew gave it, lips dropping down upon his. The kiss was slow, thorough, and left him gasping and clinging to Andrew's shoulders.

He moaned, his eyes widening. They were not alone and he was asking for this, begging for it. Max rocked back and forth, the cloth of his trousers abrading his ass. Andrew's hand curled around his backside, fingertip tapping his crack. He jumped, a frighteningly loud noise escaping him. Gracious. Here in the dining room?

Joseph chuckled softly. "Oh, I do remember those days fondly."

"Samuel is an old pro now, eh?" Andrew smiled into Max's eyes.

"I can still surprise him sometimes."

"When he works at it." Oh, there was wickedness in that corn cob of a voice.

Max laughed a little, not sure why exactly. He thought he was following the spirit of the conversation.

"Naughty boy. I would hate to punish you." Joseph's voice was full of warmth, laughter.

"No you wouldn't."

"Is this normal here?" Max asked.

"Incredibly." Andrew's eyes sparkled in the lamplight. "When one finally has the freedom to act on his desire, one tends to revel in it."

"Freedom." Max tested the word on his tongue before kissing Andrew again. He felt giddy, his earlier worry fading for now.

Andrew, for his part, seemed utterly pleased. That grin stretched his cheeks, and Max felt the heavy rise of Andrew's cock against his bottom.

Max wanted nothing more than to rub back, to offer his aching body for penetration.

"No one cares, sweet. Look at Samuel and Joseph." Samuel had slipped across to sit against Joseph's side, and they were sharing deep kisses.

"What about the others? The staff?"

"Well, Daniel is blind…" Andrew kissed his neck. "They're loyal and likeminded."

"I cannot believe that this place exists." Max hand to wonder at his luck stumbling upon Andrew and this place.

"I thought the same." Andrew petted his lower back, his thigh.

That comforted him, made him feel less like an innocent. "How long have you been a member?"

"About five years." Andrew licked his lower lip. "I was wide-eyed and amazed, even though I thought myself quite debauched."

"The thought of you wide-eyed is... more than intriguing," he admitted, and Joseph laughed.

"It was adorable, Max. Utterly."

"He's been here forever," Andrew asserted. "He vets all the new members, don't you, Joseph?"

"I do. With my boy."

Was that what this was? A test? A challenge? Were Joseph and Samuel analyzing him?

Andrew tilted his face up. "This is about you and me. Just us. I want you to be comfortable here, though, and know these are people who are on your side. Even Lionel, though he's not proving it."

"Have I offended him in some way?"

"He's been in a foul mood," Joseph murmured. "Well before today."

"I can understand that. I have been known to have a foul mood of my own."

"Lionel is sometimes prone to them. Distraction is key. Zane ought to do the trick." Andrew winked at him.

They spoke of such things so casually. "So, do you believe the man at the boarding house, Vincent, do you believe he was telling truths?"

Samuel met his eyes once more. "I do, honey. He saw something, and the rest of your spirits are real agitated. Something is up."

"Can you...can you ask them what they want?"

Samuel shook his head. "I can only see them."

"Oh." He chewed his lower lip. "Is there someone who can talk to them?"

"That would be Giles. He's rather complicated, that man." Joseph flipped a languid hand.

"He's entirely too happy about catastrophes," Max muttered.

"He likes it too much when crazy things happen."

"Ah, I see he's met Giles." Joseph's laughter was soft and wry.

"Giles went out of the club for him. For a séance."

"Really? Extraordinary."

"Is it? Why is it?" Max glanced at them all in turn.

Andrew chuckled. "He's special and in great demand. I've never seen him leave before. He told me himself he was usually too busy."

"Goodness." Max wasn't sure what to say. Giles had seemed surprised by the outside world, but surely that was an affectation. The temptation to go take Giles out, for supper, for a long walk around Mount Vernon was huge.

"You're smiling in a very evil way." Andrew stroked his cheek.

"Never. I was just thinking of taking Giles for a tour of the city. Maybe a meal at a five-cent lunch room."

"Oh, that would be a dangerous idea." Andrew couldn't seem to fight his laughter.

"But what if he wants to go out, he's just scared to do it alone?" Max hated the thought that Giles was sad and alone and putting on a brave face.

Joseph snorted. "Giles isn't afraid of anything."

He would just invite the man. Giles was an adult. He could make his mind up. Max liked the idea of introducing Giles to the world again.

"Stop plotting and kiss me," Andrew demanded.

"I can do that." He leaned down and brought their lips together.

Andrew hummed, the sound so pleased, then pushed into Max's mouth with his tongue, tasting him deeply. Suddenly the world disappeared, leaving him clinging to Andrew, wanton and needy. He couldn't breathe, couldn't see anything but his lover.

"I have you. I have you, Max."

"I know. I know." That much he was sure of. Andrew held him tight, kept him safe.

"Good."

He rocked on Andrew's thighs, his hind end stinging. The others seemed to be worlds away, because Max couldn't hear them, but he knew Joseph and Samuel were loving each other this same way.

What a world. What a strange and wonderful place he had suddenly fallen into.

When Andrew kissed him like that, all Max could do was hope he could be like Giles and never have to leave. Well, except by choice.

Andrew wiped his hands on his trousers, his nerves threatening to overtake him.

He and Max were meeting with Giles and Samuel today to begin Max's training for the position at the club. Not only did Max have to learn to control his talent, he had to learn exactly what his talent was, and involving the spirits was always unpredictable.

Especially since Max refused to consider the idea that his talents were tied to the spirit world at all. He swore all he could do was move things with his mind.

Samuel waited in the library, Joseph reading in a chair not far away. Joseph was never, ever far away from his lover. Ever watchful, Joseph kept Samuel safe, asserting that the man had endured too much already.

Andrew had been about a few times when Samuel did his work and it went badly. He had nothing but respect for Joseph and a deep regret that Samuel had the gift he had.

"Is Giles in there already, as well?" Andrew asked, Max shifting restlessly at his side.

"He is." Joseph nodded and smiled. "Good luck."

Max looked as if he might bolt.

"Easy, lad. You're going to be fine." Andrew hoped.

"I'm sure. It's one thing to know you have what you call a

talent. It's another to engage in training to hone it. To have other people acknowledge it."

"Would you feel better if we call it a séance?" he teased.

"Yes." Max nodded very seriously, but his lips twitched. "We'll be fine."

"Of course we will. Come now. This is best started."

They stepped into the library together, and Giles popped up before them, scaring Andrew half to death. "I wondered if you would just stand out there all day. Really, we need to get moving."

Samuel's husky laughter found them, and Andrew rolled his eyes. "Be good, Giles."

"We have a schedule. Samuel, I need to know what you see, please."

"There are a score of them. Layers. No one strong, but many."

"Hmm. Ages? He'll need to identify any he can. Come on, Max, sit down." It was sort of like a séance, with a round table and several chairs set up. Giles had also provided paper, pens, and ink.

"Mostly children, young. There have been fires, hmm? Many fires?"

Max went pale, and Andrew reached for Max's hand. No one had died in the fire Max accidentally set off. He'd said so.

Max's stiff lips moved. "How did you—"

"I told you. I see them. I can't not see them."

Giles settled across from them, his presence suddenly like a warm towel after a chilling rain. "There, now. Tell me, Max. About the fires."

"Which one? They follow me. I swear, I think I'm cursed."

Giles flapped a hand. "Nonsense. Spirits often try to communicate that they're with you through fire. Or perhaps protect you, if you call to other spiritual entities as well. Fire cleanses."

"It also kills," Max whispered.

"Regardless, we need to discover who you call to and assure that you don't call to those entities that are unwanted."

"How?" Max squeezed his hand so hard it ached.

Andrew squeezed back. "You must trust us, love."

"I do. I'm trying. You're serious? There are ghosts? Spirits?"

Samuel nodded, scarred throat working. "Many. They are close, pressing against you."

Max waved his hands in the air as if swatting at flies. "I— How? I can't feel them."

"Try to move this pen." Giles touched an ornate pen with gold chasing on the shaft.

Max nodded and Andrew could feel the focus, see it, and the pen slipped across the table.

"Samuel?"

"A young lad with ginger curls."

Max started. "Are you serious? I mean, you said to move it, so if there is a spirit, she heard you, not me."

Giles snorted. "Very well. Pick another object but don't tell us what it is."

Max's eyes landed on piece of paper, his lad obviously willing it to move. It took a few seconds, then the paper fluttered, then flew across the room, Samuel catching it easily.

"This is an older lad. Not yet bearded, but strapping. He looks very much like our Max."

Andrew studied Max, who looked now as if he had seen a ghost. "Does he have a scar on his upper lip?"

"He does, and clothes like a farmer."

"My brother." Max closed his eyes. "Why would he stay with me? It wasn't my fault."

"Obviously he wants to help. None of these spirits are acting against you, Max. They are helping." Giles sounded a bit as if he was speaking to a child.

Andrew poked Giles on the arm. "Be nice. This is all new."

Giles rolled his eyes, but relented. "Very well. Think of them as protective and helpful."

"The Calloway girl wasn't. She scared the bejesus out of me."

Samuel and Giles looked to Andrew, who shrugged. "He actually saw her. In his rooms."

"A warning then," Giles murmured. "I wonder of what?"

"They're moving about him. Things may start flying soon." Samuel was no help whatsoever.

Giles gave the air around Max's head a stern look. "Behave yourselves, if you please."

"I don't belong here, do I?" Max's voice was flat and dead.

"What on earth are you talking about? Samuel sees ghosts. Ignatius uses spirit guides to help him unearth secrets. We have ghost talkers and ghost hunters and mediums. So you're a real medium and not a fake. So what?" They all stared at Giles until he flushed dark red. "Not good?"

"I think it's pretty damn great." Samuel grinned, the look like a carved jack-o-lantern. "Shit, I never get anybody to listen to me. You didn't even know they were there and they followed orders."

Max searched out Andrew's eyes, and Andrew smiled his encouragement. "You're amazing, sweet."

"I don't feel amazing. I feel… less. Strange."

"Nothing is different but your perception," Giles said briskly. "Now, concentrate on something heavier but not breakable. Ask, in your mind, for it to be moved from one place to another."

This time he watched Max close his eyes, brows lowering as he concentrated. Samuel watched, black eyes following to a straight-backed chair, the man obviously observing something.

The chair rose off the floor, floating toward them. It tilted a bit, then righted in a jerky manner, before plopping down by the table.

"Very nice, girls," Samuel muttered.

"That's unnerving, you know," Max said.

"Get used to it." Samuel winked, which Andrew always found more than unnerving with those totally black demon eyes Samuel boasted.

"Very nice." Giles clapped his hands. "You see? Useful."

"What is it you want me to do for the Club, Giles? What good am I?" Max's mouth turned down at the corners, his shoulders slumped.

"Well, if nothing else you can gather up loose spirits that float through the door."

"Not helping?" Giles sighed. "I can be inappropriate. The thing is, we never know what value any talent will have until an incident occurs where we need it. I think you can be of great help to Andrew in debunking charlatans, however. Your ghosts may come in very handy when someone doesn't really want spirits about."

Andrew nodded slowly. "I can see the value in that."

"I didn't even know that's what they were. I thought I was…" Max wouldn't quite meet his eyes.

"You're perfect." Andrew pulled Max to him, holding him again on his lap. Poor Max. He was confused and worried, sad that he wasn't the mental talent he thought he was. "There's no bad here."

"Indeed. You're fascinating. Utterly fascinating. I've never met someone that drew spirits and kept them." Giles was almost bouncing.

Max looked at Giles. "Really? You mean it?"

"I do, lad! I cannot wait to work more with you. And Samuel. Andrew is the useless one here."

"Thank you, my friend." The temptation to put Giles over his knee was huge, but he feared he'd find himself turned inside out if he dared.

"Quite." Giles grinned at him, so cheerful he had to laugh.

"Are we done for the day, Giles? I think I wish to take Max to our rooms, discuss all we've learned."

"Yes, yes. Joseph, come get your boy. I have archiving to do."

Like magic, Joseph appeared and closed Samuel's eyes, a blindfold pulled from one of Joseph's waistcoat pockets. "My turn to do some training," Joseph murmured, and Andrew shivered from the intent in the words. He'd seen Joseph put Samuel through his paces.

"Do you imagine that they're awful to look upon, Andrew?" Max whispered.

"No. No, I suppose instead there are simply far more of them than we think, everywhere. It must be overwhelming for him."

"I can't imagine."

No. No, neither could Andrew, but he didn't have to worry about it. His talent lay elsewhere. So did Max's. He had a feeling there was a reason Max couldn't see or hear the spirits. They were there for a very specific reason, and Max needed them as much as they needed him.

Andrew worried about what that meant in regards to the Calloway girl.

He linked arms with Max to head back to their room.

He could only imagine the thoughts that zipped through Max's mind, the worries that filled his lad. Andrew would draw them all out, let him relieve his doubt.

"I feel more than a bit of an idiot, Andrew."

"Why? How could you know? None of us are born knowing how this works, and no one taught you." He kissed the top of Max's head.

"Still...how will I ever be able to use the WC knowing that there are spirits clinging to me? How will I be free to enjoy you?"

"The same way we did before. Luckily for you, I don't mind an audience."

"But Samuel said they were children!"

"How do you know they're always there? For all you know, they disappear when we kiss." He would spank Max silly if he said they would never make love again. "Besides, think of all they've seen. Spirits have different rules from ours, different vision."

"They do?" Max bit his lower lip, looking very young. "I don't know what to think."

"Then don't think." He shut the door behind them so he could press Max against it.

"All questions cannot be answered by drugging me with your kisses, Andrew."

"Nonsense." He kissed Max to prove it. "Though some problems are best solved with spanking."

"Stop. What if they hear you?"

"Tell them to go away. They like to do things for you. They can come back when we're done."

"As simple as that?"

"Oh, for—" He took Max's mouth again, intent on driving the worry from his lad's mind.

Max clung to him, ready, he thought, to believe. To hope, at least. That was enough for Andrew.

The spirits would watch or not, he was unconcerned. He needed his lover, needed this connection between them.

The rest of the world, or underworld, could go hang themselves.

Chapter Nine

Max couldn't quite shake the worry about the spirits watching him, clinging to him, judging him. Andrew told him that he shouldn't worry, but how, exactly, could he not?

He didn't want spirits surrounding him every day like so many fallen leaves. He wanted… well, frankly he wanted to be the talent who had so impressed Andrew when they first met.

Max peered out of his room, alone since Andrew had left for the day to attend to some business matters. "Okay, walls. Stay as you are."

It seemed ridiculous, to speak to walls, but it always appeared quite necessary. Max knew all he had to do was find a bell pull and someone would appear to lead him about, but he was quite determined to go it alone.

Lead him about…

He tilted his head. "I need to go to the dining room, spirits. Can you take me there?" Giles told him to begin asking for help since he was giving his energy to the ghosts.

He stepped forward, unsure how they could help, and walked right into a wall. Dammit!

Clenching his fists, Max breathed in deep, then let it out. Very well. He could do this on his own and to hell with all of his supposed helpers. Max lay one hand on the wall and began walking parallel.

"Mister Max?"

He damn near jumped out of his skin when Daniel's voice sounded, low and soft.

"What? Lord, you frightened me, I swear."

Daniel's empty eyes stared right through him. "Sorry, sir. I could hear you were lost. Dining room?"

"Yes, please. Since no other spirit seems willing to help me." He sounded like a petulant child and he knew it.

"Ah." There was a wealth of meaning in that single word. "I don't suppose you would welcome a suggestion?"

"Please. Please." Daniel was a ghost, wasn't he? Surely he could communicate with these ne'er do wells surrounding him.

"Perhaps you should use the skills you have already perfected?"

Max frowned, confused. "But that's not real. I mean, I was never able to move things with my mind."

"But they still are your talents, sir." Daniel spread his hands. "You had ways of communicating with them. It worked. Why change it now?"

Max's mouth dropped open. "I never even thought…"

"Of course not. Everything seemed to change, when, in fact, it had not." The expression upon Daniel's face was kind, not mocking.

"I feel out of step with the whole world." He loved Andrew so, but this openness, this loving, was something he'd never expected. Then there was the fact that he really was a medium.

"You are not the first person to express that to me. I imagine every single person entering this building experiences that same emotion. This place is... unique. Not in all the world, of course, but unique nonetheless."

"How did you come to be here?" Was that impertinent?" Max was so curious about the various inhabitants, but he didn't wish to be offensive.

Daniel frowned. "I don't really know, Mister Max. I think I have always been here."

"Always." What an idea. He couldn't fathom it — always being somewhere.

"Mmm. Here we are. If you should need me, I'm but a

thought away." Daniel smiled, really smiled, and left him at the door of the dining room.

"Thank you!" he called, then searched for a friendly face in the crowd of diners. Andrew's friend Jean waved at him, his gold pirate earrings glinting in the light.

Max grinned, waving back and walking to join the fellow and his sea captain, Isaiah. This was his life now. He could hardly credit it.

Now, if he could just get a spirit to hand him the salt cellar…

Andrew loathed accounts.

His father had managed every damned thing at the bank himself. The old fart had checked every tally, had counted every bloody coin a few times a year.

Andrew had a manager for such things. An honest man, vetted by Andrew's friend Gallagher at the club, who had an uncanny knack for knowing when a man was telling the truth.

Regardless of how honest Mr. Fallon was, Andrew still had to meet with him monthly, and today it had put him in an impatient mood. He returned to Club Raven in a rush, eager to be back with Max after a grueling day of ink and numbers.

Max fascinated him — both his talent for gathering specters to him and for the spark that seemed to bind them together.

His hands itched to touch, his cock firming at the thoughts running through his head.

Which was why he didn't see Lionel until he ran smack into his friend, nearly bowling him over.

"Good lord, do watch where you're headed. Someone will take offense!" Lionel's words were harsh, unhappy.

"Sorry." He steadied Lionel with a soft touch. "Sorry. I'm eager."

"Young love, hmm? Have you discovered his needs yet?"

Andrew nodded, because that was more the Lionel he knew,

smiling that sly little smile. "Indeed. Well, at least some of them. They match mine."

"Lucky boy! We should all have that. Compatibility is so vital."

It was so difficult to sense whether Lionel was sincere. There was some undercurrent to his words today, just as there had been at luncheon the last time they'd seen each other.

Oh, hell, Lionel was the empath, not him. Who knew what the man was thinking?

"It is. I hope you can be happy for me, Lionel."

"Why on earth wouldn't I be pleased? He seems malleable, if not particularly law-abiding."

"You seemed… unhappy. At lunch the other day." That was delicate, right? He wanted to tread carefully, but still probe whatever was bothering his friend.

Lionel shrugged, the move deceptively casual. "Unhappiness seems to be my curse, Andrew."

"It doesn't have to be so, Lionel."

Lionel snorted. "You try experiencing all the highs and lows of every person in this club every day." Those bright green eyes took on a haunted expression. "It's exhausting."

"Come to my house. Come stay there. There are only the barest staff and they would welcome you. I will be there once Max has been well-trained."

"Mmm, training." Lionel winked. "Thank you, my dear, but I shall pass. I don't want to interfere, and Max thinks I am a bastard, no doubt." Lionel's lean face seemed to relax, his frown smoothing. "I shall be back to my ironic self in no time, I'm sure."

He reached out to embrace his oldest friend, utterly shocked when Lionel stepped back. "Go to your man, Andrew. I will see you at supper, perhaps."

He drew his hands back, feeling bereft somehow. "I hope you will. Think about my offer, I mean it. My home is always open to you." Andrew forced a chuckle. "Even if it is a monstrosity."

"You're a good man, Andrew. You should know that I believe that. A good man."

"I try, my friend." He reached out then, and Lionel did touch his hand briefly, his skin feverishly hot.

"Now, go to your man." Lionel smiled faintly. "His ass is waiting for your attention."

"So delicate." Andrew paused at the foot of the stairs. "You'll tell me. If you need me. Yes?"

"If I need you." He got the briefest of nods and a look that seemed utterly lost for a moment, then Lionel left him, walking away without another glance.

Andrew stared for a few seconds, concerned. Then he turned and mounted the stairs, his mind racing.

When he got to the room he shared with Max, however, the door opened under his hand and he saw Max, sitting on the bed, reading some tome Giles had given him.

Every other thing in his mind fled before the beauty of his lover, and Andrew smiled. "Hello, sweet. I'm back."

Max's smile was all Andrew could ask for. Everything he needed.

The rest of the world would just have to go hang itself for a bit. This was their time.

Max trained with Giles and Samuel, as well as a variety of other club members, for nearly a fortnight. He still wasn't sure how to feel, but Andrew had convinced him the spirits left them when they made love, so he was willing to go on a bit of faith with everything else.

Still, when Andrew woke him early one morning, excited and bouncing, he was shocked at the words that went with Andrew's mood.

"We have an assignment outside of the club today, love."

"We do?" Fear flooded him, followed by anticipation. He

wanted to earn his keep, needed to.

"We do. Giles has decided you need a field run."

"What are we going to do? Where are we off to?"

"Near the Basin. There's a family complaining of a man who agreed to rid them of a ghost. He's not doing his job, apparently." Andrew grinned hugely.

"Oh?" Was it a true spirit or just a charlatan in all ways? He itched to discover the truth.

"Yes, you see now. It's an addiction, the job we do here. I can feel you vibrate."

"So do we simply invite ourselves as you did with me?"

"The family spoke to one of our members. Just as a friend, you understand. He got us invited." Andrew stroked his back.

"Right. Should I wear my deep mourning or light?"

"Light, I believe. The ghost is a relatively old one, but we should be respectful."

Max chuckled. He only had the choice the last few days, since the tailor had delivered him three new suits of clothing.

"Is it unseemly to be excited?" He hadn't been out of the club in a fortnight.

"Not a bit. It's good to get out and stretch our mental muscles." Andrew's blue eyes sparkled.

"Yes." Even if his were spiritual in truth. He examined that thought, and it didn't hurt as much as it had a few weeks ago. The club members welcomed him with open arms, even if his meeting with each of the owners had felt… chilly. Or brusque, in the case of the Tony one.

Of course, they must be busy, with so many things under their purview. Who was he to judge? They ran a club that actually seemed alive. It changed and grew, tricked the eye and the mind. At least Max could get to his room alone now.

Most of the time, at any rate.

On occasion he had to call for Daniel, who proved to be a gem of a man and who couldn't see the illusions the club threw their way.

Once he'd discovered that, he'd taken to bringing one of his orbs and trusting that his newly discovered friends wouldn't lead him astray. They never did, either, which made accepting the loss of his old talent more acceptable.

Andrew slapped his hip, making it sting. "Up, love. We're on a case!"

"Will Giles be coming with us?"

"Not today. If we need him, I'm sure he will be happy to come along, but today is reconnaissance." Andrew kissed him before rolling off the bed. He wore only his shirt and trousers.

The temptation to reach up and squeeze was huge. Oh, why not? Andrew was his lover. He could touch.

He allowed his hands their head, so to speak, and took himself a double handful of man.

"Max!" Andrew stood, whirling about, laughter ringing out. "Naughty."

"I'm sure I don't know what you're talking about!" he protested, laughing along with his lover.

"No? I can show you later." Those blue eyes went dark, heated.

"Please. A reward for a job well done?"

"Absolutely. Your ass needs color."

"Andrew!" His body took immediate notice and he popped his cock none too gently. "After work."

"Mmm." Andrew patted his butt before turning back to the washbasin.

Soon enough they were both dressed and on their way to the Basin area. The family's home was slim, tall, and older than he would have expected.

He felt a rush of anger — partially born from shame, he imagined, because this was him, not so long ago. Still, this was no family resting upon a vast fortune, not in this house. At least Max had the decency to relieve only people who had money to spare.

Andrew squeezed his elbow, guiding him up the stairs to knock.

A young man answered, clearly a family member. No servants.

"Misters Bellame and Meechum," Andrew said. "You're expecting us."

"Yes, sirs. Please. Mother is waiting in the drawing room with Mister Hannity and my aunts."

"Thank you." Andrew stepped in and removed his hat. Max followed his lead. "Mr. Hannity is the medium?"

"Yes, sir. Mother is quite...enthralled."

"I can only imagine." Andrew looked to Max. "People do love to feel special."

Max nodded seriously, hoping he was taking the right cue. "I have some experience in these matters."

"Do you?"

"Indeed." He allowed himself to be the Mesmerizing Maximillian, the act as comfortable as his favorite coat. "I look forward to meeting my compatriot. Perhaps I can add my expertise to his."

"Hmm." The young man chewed his lip. "Well, if you're ready."

"What's your name?" Andrew asked.

"Jeffrey."

"It's a pleasure to meet you. We were sent by Master Devins, your father's friend."

Those eyes lit up. "Ah. Good, good. Come on." He led the way into the parlor, seeming much relieved.

Max looked over to Andrew, pleased that this time the man worked on the same side he did. They could uncover this together.

Mr. Hannity was a small, dapper man with a waxed beard and kohl around his eyes. He wore a turban, but a cold reading told Max he was from somewhere near him. New York City, perhaps.

He held himself to his full height and made a bow, using his gifts — *his ghosts?* — to make himself seem a bit larger, more impressive.

"Good afternoon, ladies and gentlemen. I'm Maximillian.

How do you do?" Showtime.

Mr. Hannity stared down at him over a long, thin nose. "Pardon me? Emma? Who is this?"

Emma? Oh, if the man was calling her familiar, there was an issue indeed.

"A friend of the family," Jeffrey murmured. "And his companion. Misters Meechum and Bellame."

The lady of the house—who was either deep in her cups or given enough laudanum to make her eyes droop in an alarming manner—blinked at them owlishly. "Do I know you, gentlemen?"

"Indeed you do, madam. Master Devens sent us to assist in your time of need."

"Need what?" Hannity raised a carefully groomed brow. "I am all the help she requires."

"And yet you have not handled the pesky spirit," Andrew said gently.

"Tell me of your…" A sudden image appeared in the center of his brain—a strapping young man with a happy smile, hair the same straw as the son that had opened the door. In the dust upon the table, the name Jeremiah appeared. "Jeremiah."

The lady started, her eyes widening. She clutched the chest of her gown. "Yes! You know!"

"The spirits are with me, madam, always."

He swore he heard a titter. Andrew needed to hush. Maybe it wasn't Andrew…

Hannity stood, eyes flashing with ire. "Now, see here…"

He didn't respond, he simply stood, quiet and still. He knew all the tricks, all the fakes. He didn't have to pretend. Much. Especially not now.

A gusty sigh sounded, and Hannity sank to the settee once more. "Yes, well. I have had difficulty."

"Perhaps I can lend a hand. He was a comely lad, hmm?"

"Yes. Golden like my Jeffrey." The missus sniffed. "He's been gone some years, and only recently returned."

"How recently?" Andrew asked, sinking into a chair and accepting a cup of tea.

"Easter. I swear to you, I can hear his voice, singing to me."

"Ah." Max knew that meant nothing, but people liked thinking noises.

"She's been hoping to understand what he wishes to tell her," Hannity said, and Max nodded. That was the most challenging job, because what you needed to discover was what the client to hear.

Andrew watched, eyes bright. He wore this tiny smile Max remembered well, and he was glad it was directed at Hannity.

He cleared his throat, closed his eyes, and held up his hands, palms up. "Jeremiah. What is it you wish to tell us?"

The vase on the side table began to slide, scraping along the veneer.

"Oh, no! Jeffrey."

At the lady's cry, the son leaped forward to catch the vase before it fell.

Jeremiah. He thought hard, trying to sense whether his particular spirits sensed the boy.

A small knickknack on the table next to Hannity exploded, throwing shards of porcelain on the man, causing him to jump up in terror.

"It seems Jeremiah does not approve, sir," Andrew drawled, voice thick as syrup.

"Stop it." Hannity clenched his hands into fists. "Whatever you're doing, stop it!"

Suddenly Max could see a handprint pressing into Hannity's throat. Goodness. Someone was angry.

"Jeremiah, I can help you." He said it solemnly, with great weight. He wasn't sure exactly what was happening, but he knew that the spirits fed off him, Giles had said so.

The handprint disappeared, and Hannity gasped, holding his throat. "You're mad."

"Pardon me? Are you ill, sir? Do you require assistance?"

Max raised his brows with what he hoped was alarm.

Andrew sprang to his feet. "Water, dear sir?"

"Stay back. You...you wish to harm me!"

"Nonsense." Andrew's voice was so firm, steady as anything. "You've taken ill, sir."

"Emily—"

The lady in question stared at Hannity, her face pale. "He wanted to hurt you. Why?"

"Emily, dearest—"

Andrew gasped, the sound comically loud. When all eyes turned to him, he clapped a hand over his mouth. "Your pardon. Such familiarity shocked me."

Oh, little shit. Max adored him. "I vow, Mr. Hannity must be ill."

"Indeed. I shall take him to—do you have a study, sir?" Andrew asked the man of the house.

"We do. Follow me." Said man of the house held himself in a way that screamed disapproval.

"Immediately." Andrew rose, swept Hannity up like a man scooping up a chicken, and rushed him from the room.

Max moved to sit on the settee so he could speak earnestly with Mrs. Faircloth. "Madame, I must tell you, your Jeremiah thinks Mr. Hannity is seeking to bilk you of your jewels." The red glass in the curio cabinet turned slowly, silently. "Your garnets or rubies, perhaps?"

"I have Elie rubies. The only thing left from my mother. They're actually garnets, and they came from Scotland. They're quite rare." She sniffed, her chin quivering. "He seemed so helpful."

"And adoring." He nodded when her eyes flew wide, adding gently, "It's lovely to have someone pay attention, isn't it?"

Her lips pursed with the effort to hold her emotions in and he felt for her, he did, but Hannity would leave her bare and desperate to explain to her husband what had happened.

"I miss him so."

"I know you do, but you have a living son who would help you, and Jeremiah is here with you, guiding you."

"My husband wants him banished. That's why George came in the first place."

George. Wearing a turban. Good gad.

"We'll ask him to quiet himself then, not disturb the master of the house."

"Can we do that?"

Max smiled, hoping he was right. "We just did."

"You are a comfort, Mister…?"

"Maximillian works more than well enough, madame."

"Are you a showman, Maximillian? You have a way about you."

"I do have a penchant for drama, but I'm also quite good at what I do."

"What do I owe you for your assistance, sir?"

"Nothing." He dared to reach out and touch her hand lightly. "I came to help because a friend of your family asked me to." The club was paying his way now.

"Please don't tell my husband what a fool I've been…"

"Not a word." He shook his head gravely, and she smiled, he lips trembling less.

"Thank you. You're a dear."

"I fear Mr. Hannity was indisposed and we found him a cab." Andrew stepped back into the room, Mr. Faircloth behind him. "He said he knew he was outclassed, and if you need a medium, you should call upon Maximillian here. I imagine things will quiet down considerably."

"Mister Maximillian insists that Jeremiah is settled in his soul, indeed."

"Good, good." Andrew smiled at him, cheerful as a lark.

"Will you stay for tea?"

"Not today, I think," Andrew said. "If you should need us, here is our direction." Andrew handed a card to the elder Mr. Faircloth.

"I am in your debts, sirs."

"Never say so."

Max had to admit, Andrew was so different than he had been at Max's séances that it was night and day. Once Jeffrey had shown them out, he poked Andrew's arm. "This is what you do? Why did you not expose me?"

"Because you had a real talent. And because both of the men of the houses you were at were complicit."

"I never took advantage, Andrew. I swear to you. I never took what wasn't freely offered."

"No, I knew that about you right away." Andrew lowered his voice. "And I wanted you."

"At first sight? Truly?"

"Yes. You fascinated me so that I rather ignored my job. Still, I think you did both families I saw you with some good."

He refused to be ashamed. He had been paid for a service, to bring peace to the family. At least he hadn't burned down their house.

"Come along, Max."

"Back to the club?" He found his feet dragging, even though Andrew had promised him a reward.

"No. No, I believe we should go home."

"Home?" He tugged Andrew to a stop. "I live at the club."

"And I have been of late, but I have a house. Come along. You should see it. It's a monstrosity."

Oh. Oh, how fascinating. "I'm intrigued."

"You'll be appalled, no doubt. My father was the one who built it and decorated it. It's entirely overblown. Writhing baroque glory, neo-classic columns, Asian decoratives." Andrew shuddered. "All populated with the huge, dark furniture so popular a few years back."

"It doesn't seem like you, Andrew. Not at all, if I'm honest."

"Shall we take the horsecar?" Andrew drew him to the rail stop, the horse drawn streetcars running on rails making a quieter ride than a cab. They settled in, making their way back toward the Mt. Vernon area where Club Raven sat.

Max leaned back on the seat, pondering the change his world had taken in the last season. How had this come to pass, that he was in a horsecar, heading to his lover's home after dealing with a specter?

Andrew took his hand since they were quite alone at this time of day, not letting go until a grumpy German lady joined them a few stops shy of Andrew's home.

They disembarked, and indeed, Andrew's home was quite grand, a stately monster detached from the surrounding homes, surrounded by an iron fence and tall trees.

Andrew saw his expression and laughed. "Indeed! Still, who's going to buy such a place? I might as well keep it."

Max felt hugely daring as he leaned close and whispered. "Think of what wickedness we can get up to in there, sir."

"There are enormous seats in every room. Wait until you see the master bedroom. It's a feat of amazing bad taste." Andrew took his hand once they were inside, a silent serving lad opening the door and closing it after them.

Andrew tugged him into a parlor that looked like something out of a Tudor nightmare, then kissed him full on the mouth.

He stiffened in shock, but only for a moment, then he pushed close, hand coming to rest on Andrew's waist. The kiss stunned him into stillness, the intensity of it roaring between them. His cock hardened, his hips bucking.

"Come upstairs, Max. I owe you a reward. I owe myself one as well."

The dark promise in Andrew's words stole his breath and he nodded, most embarrassingly eager.

They pelted up the stairs like giddy schoolboys, the newel posts carved to resemble the deadly sins. Gracious.

"Was the artist forbidding or directing, Andrew?"

"I think my father wanted to scare me into behaving." Andrew laughed, rubbing Lust's lewdly protruding tongue. "Sadly, I much preferred sin. I imagine that helped drive him to his early grave."

"I do seem to approve of your particular sins."

"Do you, love?" Andrew dragged him into a room with a full tester bed, the hangings on the wall all depicting battle scenes.

He burst out laughing, tickled by the very manliness of it. "That is…"

"A monstrosity?"

"I would have said ornate, but yes. Quite."

"The bathing room is lovely. Big copper tub. Mermaids and men in Italian mosaic. This room makes me glad the bed has a lid on it." Andrew began stripping him down, tearing the clothing from him. He helped, eager to save his collars and cuffs if nothing else.

They were new, after all.

Andrew threw off his own clothing, then moved to rummage in a dresser. "I swear I have… Ha!"

He came away from the drawer with a razor strop.

Max's eyes went wide, so hard and fast that they pulled at the corners. "Oh."

"You've had the strap, sweet. This is broader, somewhat harder, but I would never use it on your cock or between your cheeks. This is best applied to buttocks and thighs."

He would feel that for days, deep near his bones. "I'll never sit again."

"Of course you will. For a day or two. Then I'll take after you again." Andrew slapped the strop against his palm. "So, go to the foot of the bed and grab the two main posts." When he obeyed, Andrew tangled his fingers in Max's hair, tugging his head back. "After the strap, I'll use my hand, finish you off in the best way, hmm?"

Max caught his breath, the urge to nod making the roots of his hair twinge at the scalp. "Please."

They had tried a variety of implements: a hairbrush, a paddle, the strap. All of them gave him great pleasure, but the intimate touch of Andrew's hand filled him with joy.

"You have my word. Be a good lad and take this and I will give you everything you crave."

"Yes, Andrew." He bent, holding the posts, and stuck his ass out behind, giving Andrew an easy target. His cheeks heated, his ears burning. He needed this, and his lover had taught him not to be ashamed. Somehow together they had found something they both craved.

Andrew hit him with the strap, and it was the sound which made him jump, not so much the feel. This was a dull ache, not the sharp sting of the small strap. The second blow echoed inside him, the thud making him grunt.

They began slowly, each slap falling on a different area of skin. One in the center of each cheek. One at the top of each thigh. Then one just where thigh met butt, lifting him up on his toes.

He would feel that for days, the ache burning throughout him.

Max panted, his vision filled with the crimson bed cover, his ass beginning to burn. His balls swung every time the strop pushed him forward before he pressed back out with his hips to take the next smack.

"Lovely boy. You dance for me, express your need beautifully."

Such praise. It made his body sway, the motions bigger, more obvious. He wagged his bottom back and forth, counting each stripe Andrew laid down in his mind. His prick was hard as nails, dripping with his hunger, and he spread his thighs wider, making room for his swinging balls.

"That's it. God, you're lovely. I adore the way your skin takes color. Pink at first, then as I layer on the blows, bright red. You make me hard, Max, make me ache."

"Please, Andrew. Your hand? Soon? I've been good."

"I know you have." Andrew tossed the strap aside and flung Max bodily on the bed, making him bounce and flail as the world whirled by in a blur. "Hands and knees, sweet."

He scrambled to comply, his aching cock catching on the duvet and making it buzz. Max moaned, dipping his head, his butt sticking up.

Andrew hummed, a sound he had come to know as approval. Then the spanking began again, Andrew's hand rising and falling, slapping him madly. This time there was no protecting his hole, the tender skin behind his sac.

Andrew made sure to touch every part of him, the most tender spots getting the most attention. Max cried out, crawling up the bed toward the massive headboard, but Andrew jumped on the bed to follow him, not letting him escape for a moment.

"Shall I give you my hand here?"

A heavy blow rocked his prick, and he cried out, arching for another. His balls pulled up, and he didn't know what to do, where to go. Finally Max simply rolled to his back, grabbed his knees, and spread them, begging Andrew to take him.

"Wanton." Andrew cupped his balls in a blistering touch, rolling them, one finger tapping his hole.

"Andrew!" His breath left him in a huff, his ears ringing. He could barely breathe, and Andrew seemed just as eager, never leaving him to find oil. Andrew used spit instead, and Max groaned when two fingers slid inside him. He bore down, the sting delicious and making him hiss. "More."

"Demanding boy."

"Yes! I need you, love."

"Good." Andrew worked him open, more careful than he felt he needed, but he appreciated the love Andrew gave him.

Andrew used his other hand to slick his cock with more spit so they could slide together, Andrew's rigid length filling him. He felt every single hair on Andrew's thighs, his burning skin so sensitive that he could scream.

"Oh." Andrew stared down a him, blue eyes burning hotter than any sunny summer sky. "Max. Oh, love, you're on fire for me. I could stay right here always."

"I crave this—to ache for you." Wicked and odd, but Andrew insisted that they were lucky, to have joint needs.

"I want to give you everything." Andrew began moving faster, thighs and pelvis slapping against all the tender spots the strop had discovered.

He found himself grinding down, encouraging each and every sting. With Andrew he felt alive, amazing. Loved.

Andrew grunted, thrusts becoming short and sharp. Not long now.

"Touch me, love. Please. Touch me." He needed to spend, needed to be pushed over the edge.

Andrew reached down and grabbed his cock, jerking at it three or four times before slapping it hard enough at the base to make a clapping sound.

That was all he needed and he shot, strings of pearly seed spraying up over his belly, his chest.

Andrew shouted, grabbing Max's hips in a steely grip and thrusting hard and deep into him. Three or four sharp movements and he felt Andrew release inside him, hot and wet, filling him up.

He sucked in a shuddering breath, his entire world tightened to the heaviness inside him, the burn on his skin.

Andrew held tight to him, chest heaving, that blue stare keeping him snared. He could only look back, feeling desired. Needed.

His lover leaned forward and took a long, deep kiss, which Max returned wholeheartedly. Hilarious as the house might be, its owner meant more to him than anything had in a long, long time.

More than he would have imagined anything could.

Chapter Ten

Andrew rang for breakfast the next morning feeling pleasantly sore, his whole body filled with a delicious lassitude. He had no doubt that they would get a stern talking to at the club for not reporting in, but Max had needed time away. Time with Andrew.

Time to explore the parts of them that had nothing whatsoever to do with spirits or talents or anything but need.

He stretched, grinning when he saw Max's ass, which was exposed, and which his chamber… well, Kenneth was no maid, but he wasn't really a valet either. At any rate, Kenneth would have seen it when he answered the bell.

His marks.

The idea pleased him unmercifully.

He slid a hand over the back of Max's thigh. "Love? Breakfast soon."

Max arched for him, moaned deliciously. "What's for breakfast?"

"Oh, I imagine Kenneth and Cook will come up with a vast array. They're so pleased to have us here."

"Do you stay home often?"

"Before you came along? About half the time. Once you're trained, I can see coming here more."

"We have delicious freedom here."

"We do. And while I adore the club and our friends, I will want time alone with you." He rolled off the bed so he could toss Max a dressing gown.

Max stood there, staring at him as if he were magical.

"What?" Andrew struck a pose. "You like what you see?"

"I love you, Andrew. Most dearly."

His whole body warmed, his heart kicking into a beat that nearly choked him. He met those gray eyes, and he realized Max meant it.

"Oh, sweet. I love you, too."

Max nodded, then pulled on the robe, the silk brushing his skin.

Andrew donned his robe as well before returning to Max's side, drawn there by the smile he knew was just for him.

"Is your home haunted with spirits like the club? Or is your staff flesh and blood?"

"They're very real. They're also carefully chosen. The only one left of my father's familiars is the solicitor, and obviously he doesn't live here."

"No, that would be uncomfortable. You and your father were not close?"

"He disapproved of me. I refused to behave." Andrew snuggled up, Max's warm body calling to him. "However, I did prove to be valuable in his banking endeavors, so we made a sort of peace before he died."

"Good. So many people war with their loved ones and then regret it."

Yes, he imagined Max heard dozens and dozens of those tales.

"What of your family?" Andrew asked, curious to know all.

"My mother was a gentlewoman. My father was a ne'er do well. They're both gone. I told you about my brother and the fire."

"Yes. You have been alone for too long, hmm?"

"I have." Max kissed his chin, morning whiskers rough.

"Mmm. I should shave you, sweet."

"I would trust you. You have a steady hand."

So practical, his Max.

"Would you? I will have hot water and soap brought up."

"Yes." Max nodded easily. He supposed Max's spirits could save that pretty face if need be. Still, the easy trust suited him, honored him down to the bone.

"Breakfast, sir." Kenneth knocked gently at the door before entering, tray in hand.

"Leave it at the table, Kenneth. Can you send up hot water and shaving soap?"

"Yes, sir."

Max straightened up and went to Kenneth, holding out one hand. "Good morning. I'm Max. Pleasure to meet you."

Kenneth raised his gray brows, but smiled and took Max's hand in his gloved one. "Good morning, Mr. Max. Is there anything else you prefer? I brought coffee and chocolate, but there may be milk or juice."

"No. No, that sounds amazing. I just wanted to make introductions, that's all."

"Well, welcome."

Andrew had to stifle a grin. Kenneth hated guests, hated the extra work. Max had won him over so immediately. His lover had a fine way with people.

"Thank you." Max didn't hide his smile, not one bit.

Kenneth turned to leave them, and Andrew settled at the ornate round table with the dragon center support where he ate many a breakfast. His chamber was large enough to have all the house's furniture in it, really.

"The food smells delicious."

"Cook is inspiring. Come on, sweet." Andrew lifted covers. Eggs. Rashers of bacon. Sausages. Breads of three kinds… Cook must have been up and busy since about six am.

Max's eyes went wide, the expression impressed, and he had to admit, he was just as stunned. There were even pots of clotted cream and jam, syrups and honey.

"Gracious," Max said. "They went all out."

"Very much. I suppose Cook had no idea what you liked. She usually sends me a hard cooked egg and some porridge." He winked, then made a face.

"I don't mind the occasional gruel, but this is far superior."

"Far." Such hot, crisp bacon. Lovely. He crunched a piece, humming at the flavor. He knew Kenneth would give them ample time to eat before appearing magically with water and soap. Max devoured a fat, raisin studded pastry, then offered him one of the same.

"Mmm. This is new." He must really send his compliments to Cook.

"It's amazing. I thought Club Raven had a good chef."

"They do." Andrew shook his head. Perhaps his people were really bored. He would start to spend more time at home. With Max.

Max fed him a bite of bacon, a bit of cheese, a sweet. He returned the favor, letting Max taste the German sausages his cook preferred, the creamy eggs.

Soon his lover was in his lap, brazen as anything, warm ass snuggled against his thigh. He loved Max's willingness, his openness. Andrew had dreamed of such a connection, had hoped, but had begun to despair of finding it. Now somehow he'd been offered all he'd desired and more.

A soft knock at the door made him start. "Yes, Kenneth?"

"A message for you from your club, sir." Now Kenneth sounded long suffering.

Given that meant that those notes always meant him calling for his good shoes and coat and leaving the staff with nothing to do again, he supposed he understood.

"Thank you, Kenneth." He rose so he could take the folded note off the salver.

Max watched him with an eagle's eyes, and Andrew sighed a bit. "Giles wants our report. I'll send him a note saying we'll be there around luncheon."

"We can return after, yes? Your bed is most welcoming."

"We can and will." He stroked Max's hand where it lay on the table. "First we must make you presentable."

"That may take more than a razor and a strop, Andrew."

"Ha! Kenneth had your clothing pressed. We'll get you a few more day suits as things progress."

"I can pay for them."

"Nonsense. I have enough for both of us until you begin to grow a nest egg, hmm? Indulge me. I've never had a lovely man to dress as I will before."

Max flushed beautifully, and Kenneth's little assistant… Oh, what was his name? He appeared with water and soap and Andrew's straight razor, already sharpened to a gleaming perfection.

"Thank you." He waved the boy off, then grinned at Max, knowing the expression was wolfish and hungry. "Off with the robe, dearest."

"The robe isn't in the way of my chin whiskers, you know?"

"Who says I intend to stop there?" His grin widened at Max's shocked expression. So many firsts to explore.

He reached inside the robe and tugged Max's short hairs hard enough to make his lover gasp. "I wish to play, Max. I wish to see you in your trousers at the club and know that you are sensitive, hard, aching."

"Andrew! I can't… I mean. Oh, damn." Max untied the robe and sat back in his chair, legs spreading. "Anything."

"That is, as always, the perfect answer." He reached down and cupped Max's heavy sac, rolling the sensitive orbs in his fingers.

Max grunted, eyes wide.

"Mmm. We should start with your bristly chin, though, just so you'll know I can do this without harming you." Andrew squeezed what he held before letting go so he could wet a towel and lay it across Max's lower face. "Imagine, though, how this heated towel will feel on your lap."

Max moaned. "My ass is already so hot I can hardly bear it."

"Tonight I will have you hold yourself open so I can whip your shaved hole." He was having a ball.

"I can't! You can't shave me there, can you?"

"Watch me." Andrew lifted the towel, then wetted it again while the water was hot. He placed it over Max's more than a bit interested privates before whipping up a lather with the soap.

Max bucked in the chair, eyes rolling as he threw his head back and exposed his throat.

"That's perfect, love." He applied the foam to Max's skin, getting it good and soapy so this would go easily. "Now hold still, hmm?"

"Yes, lover." Max moaned for him, sweet as amber honey.

He opened the razor, steeling himself to have steady hands and a smooth, easy motion with the shaving. He wanted this to be pleasurable for them both.

He wanted his beloved to let him bare that heavy cock and know that the fabric of Max's clothes chafed unbearably.

Carefully, ever so slowly, Andrew dragged the razor over the softened beard on Max's face. He wiped the razor on the towel, then did it again and again, careful not to nick anything.

"Love. So intimate."

Max had no idea. The other shaving would leave Max begging to come…

He finished with Max's face easily, proud of his barber-like skills.

"Now your lower belly, hmm? Just to lead up to the main act."

"Andrew. You were serious?"

Yes, and Max was hard as diamonds. That would actually help keep things out of the way. No loose skin.

"I am. This was done to me once, and I almost died from the feel of my bare skin where I had not been bare in so long." He left Lionel's name out of it, not wanting to spoil the mood.

Every teacher was once a student, weren't they?

Max watched him with drugged eyes as he carefully trimmed away the heaviest curls with a tiny pair of silver shears. The *snip snip* sound was wickedly arousing, and he leaned back before he began to work his magic with the razor. The black curls had been reduced to stubble and Max's cock looked angry, red-tipped and needy.

Andrew licked his lips, knowing he would suck Max once the soap was gone, once those heavy balls and the tight asscrack were clean, too.

"Come, hook your legs over the arms of the chair, beloved, and scoot down to the edge of the cushion."

Max moved with alacrity, sliding down, lifting and spreading. God in heaven, that looked decadent. Perverse.

Then he began to apply the soap, using the bristles of the beaver brush to ease his way. He soaped Max's balls as well as the base of that sweet cock so all would be ready. Andrew glanced up, staring into Max's gray eyes. "Are you ready to be very, very still?"

"As you wish, Andrew."

His cock firmed even more, and he took Max's dick in one hand, the other wielding the razor. He scraped away the hairs, pulling back when Max moaned and shook. Once Max stilled he began again, baring the entire area before rinsing Max off.

Then he bent to the most delicate work, denuding the tiny hairs from Max's hole, from the strip of skin between it and Max's newly naked sac.

Max cried out for him, and the scent of his lover's need began to make itself known.

"Shh. Very dangerous here, love." He ran the razor up from the very middle, and Max held his breath, his body not moving a bit.

"There, now." Andrew cleaned the razor one last time, then surveyed his work. He would do Max's chest in a few days, always keeping his lover off balance. What a perfect game.

He wiped Max down with a towel, surveying his handiwork. Then he ran a finger over those heavy balls.

Max's legs drew up, as if his touch was attached to a string.

Andrew moaned, touching that tiny strip of skin he'd bared

between ass and sac. "So clean."

"Andrew…"

"Mmhmm?"

"Please."

The soft plea made his balls draw up.

"Yes, sweet." He took pity on them both, bending to wrap his lips around the tip of Max's cock. He'd set the razor aside, so he slipped both hands under Max's well-beaten ass and lifted him up.

The scent of soap and need promised to become Andrew's favorite addiction.

He licked, then sucked down lower, working until he could touch newly shaved skin with his lips. Oh, smoother than silk, the bare skin seemed to kiss his lips in return.

Max moaned, arching up, muscles tight under his hands. He slipped one finger between those muscled asscheeks, feeling the sweetness of the shaven skin. He knew it had to tingle, to burn, and he pushed a bit further.

"Please," Max said again, lifting up, panting. Begging him.

He pushed his finger against Max's hole, knowing it would be enough to push his lover to the edge.

He swallowed hard as he felt his lover's cock swell, spreading his lips wider.

"Yes!" Max shouted the word, seed pouring down his throat just like that. Sweet man. He took every drop, then slowly backed away.

When Max opened his eyes they held a dazed expression, but Max reached for him, generous and wanting to touch him.

"Mmm." He scooted to straddle Max's thighs, open his robe to rub against smooth skin.

"Andrew. I want to touch you."

"Absolutely, sweet. Anything."

Max pushed one hand between them, fingers wrapping tight around his prick and tugging him.

He worked up and down, fucking Max's fist, his need riding

him hard. All that touching, all that smooth, wonderful skin…

"My boy," he moaned. "My own."

"Yours," Max agreed, one thumbnail scraping over his flesh. That bare sting was all he needed, lightning sliding down his spine and shooting from his cock. He spent himself hard, rocking back and forth while taking the kiss he so desperately wanted, painting Max with his seed.

Finally they rested, panting together, their foreheads pressed against each other.

"You're really going to make me go to the club like this, aren't you?" Max finally asked.

"I am. You'll be mad for me by the time we can do this again," Andrew said.

"Evil man. I do adore you." That smile told him so much, Max easy in his skin, touching Andrew easily, love shining there.

"As I do you." He climbed to his feet. "Come along, Max. Time to report."

"Indeed. Work awaits!" Max sprang out of the bed, ginning hugely. Yes, Andrew imagined Max loved this, having a place, a job to do. Perhaps even someone to do it with.

Andrew knew that had done wonders for his outlook on life.

They dressed and pelted downstairs, Kenneth standing like a dour statue by the door. "We'll return this evening, Kenneth."

"Shall I have Cook prepare supper?"

"Please do! We'll have a light luncheon."

"If it's like breakfast, it will be amazing." Max patted Kenneth's arm, making the butler jump.

Oh, Max was going to make this most fun.

Andrew couldn't wait to see what he did next.

"I'll be just a moment," Andrew told Max when they reached the club. "I need to speak to Charles there privately. I'll introduce you later." Andrew lowered his voice. "Walk around a bit. Enjoy the cloth against your skin."

"Andrew, be nice." There was nothing decent about his lover. Nothing.

"I am. I am very, very nice to my lover." Andrew slipped away, leaving Max shifting from foot to foot, feeling everything rub.

"You act as if you have some disease, good man. Do be still." Lionel growled softly, the sound making him jump.

Max turned to stare at Lionel, who seemed… somehow leaner. More stark, his hair more silver.

"I'm so sorry I offended you." Max couldn't help but snap the words. He wanted to feel bad for Lionel, but he just couldn't. He knew it was jealousy, that Lionel had known Andrew when he hadn't, but he couldn't help it.

"This is a gentleman's club. You would do well to remember that."

"Yes?" Max snorted. "So would you. A gentleman knows when to move on." God, he sounded waspish. Max straightened his shoulders. "Apologies. That was out of line. Must we be enemies, Lionel? I'm sure Andrew would like us to be friends."

The man's expression seemed to soften, and there was a hint of a smile. "I have no wish to be your enemy, lad."

"Good." He smiled back. "I'm glad to hear it." Thank goodness. He thought perhaps he had defused that situation.

"Are you having a good conversation, my dears?" Andrew came up, one hand landing on his hip.

"Yes." Lionel winked broadly at Max. "You know I'm utterly charming and irresistible."

"Completely. Modest as well."

"I am." Lionel batted his lashes, but something flashed in his eyes, something he wasn't sure Andrew saw.

"We're here to meet with Giles. Would you like to have a light luncheon with us afterward?"

"I would." Lionel glanced back to Max. "I shall look forward to it."

Lionel's eyes dragged over him, the look almost offensive, disgusted as well as lecherous.

Max's mouth dropped open. Was he imagining this? Lionel had been almost friendly, he thought. Now the tide was back on the side of ugliness.

"Max? Beloved? Are you well?"

Was he? Was he well?

Lionel winked at him and moved on, so Max drew Andrew aside. "Is Lionel feeling poorly?"

"Why would you ask that, love?" Andrew frowned.

"He seems...he seems to find me an adversary."

"Nonsense." Andrew tugged him toward the stairs. "He can be brusque, but he would never look down on you."

"I'm not imagining it. He's simmering with anger." It made Max itch, made the wind move around them, ruffling his hair.

Andrew glanced back and so did Max, but Lionel was nowhere to be seen. "I'll speak to him before luncheon if you like."

"Please? I'd hate to cause upset unintentionally." Usually when he was offensive, he meant every second of it.

"Of course." Andrew pulled him aside on the landing to take a kiss. "Thank you for trying to befriend him. Lionel is not easy, but I have known him a long time."

"You've been close to him, I know." And the monster that was jealousy popped up yet again.

"I have, but it was never a love match. I adore him, but I love you so much." Andrew stroked his cheek. "Trust me?"

"With my soul."

He swore he heard a low growl, deep and ripping through the air. He turned, confused, concerned. "What was that?"

Andrew lifted his head. "I didn't hear anything, sweet."

"Odd. Are you…" There it was again, a sound that was pure animal, pure evil. "Andrew?"

Andrew opened his mouth to answer, brows drawing together when Max stumbled back toward the head of the stairs.

"Max?" Andrew reached for him.

"Andrew!" Max felt hands tugging at him. No. No, not hands. Claws. Claws digging into his upper arms and pulling him. He flew backward until he dangled in the open space over the stairwell, his legs kicking a nothing but air. Then he crashed down and rolled to the bottom of the staircase, feeling every single bump along the way.

"Max!" Andrew charged down the stairs. "Someone call Halliwell!"

"Andrew! Something's got me!" Max slid across the floor backward, his heels digging in, trying to find purchase.

"Max!" Andrew lunged for him again, fingers grazing his ankle.

"Help me!" He sent the words to the spirits that Samuel insisted lived all about him, and suddenly he surged forward, his arms feeling as if they would be tugged off.

"Help us!" Andrew shouted, and members arrived from all over, tripping over each other.

Just when he felt as if he was on the rack and his bones would break, his joints popping from their sockets, there was a flash of light and a bang that created smoke that reminded Max of brimstone. Giles was there, shouting something in Latin, and whatever it was that held him let go.

He blinked at his lover, thinking that this was not the afternoon he'd hoped for. That was about all he thought before his body insisted that the emptiness of unconsciousness was preferable to incredible pain.

Chapter Eleven

Nothing is broken or dislocated," Benjamin Halliwell finished his examination of Max and sat back to close his medical bag. "He'll be very sore, and he has some bruises. What concerns me are the claw marks on his back and shoulders. There was nothing in the room that could account for those."

Andrew nodded, staring at his lover, who had yet to regain consciousness. "It was some kind of demonic entity, I vow."

"That is beyond my purview. I'm a physician for the body." Benjamin was always so serious. Andrew understood. The war has been hard on all of them in one way or another.

"Yes, of course. Thank you, Ben."

"Call for me if anything changes." Ben rose, turning toward the door, showing the twisted, scarred side of his face.

Max lay there, pale as milk, still and quiet.

"I will."

As soon as Ben stepped out, Giles entered the room. "Tell me everything."

Andrew blinked. "We were talking about Lionel being out of sorts. I kissed him, but then something pulled him off the steps and threw him down."

"Did he say anything else, give any warning?"

"He said something had him." The terror on Max's face when he was flung into thin air would stay with Andrew for a long while. "He complained of a sound, perhaps? I didn't hear it."

"Hmm." Giles nodded sharply. "I will sit with him. You go and see Lionel."

"What? Why?"

"Because he spoke to Max last. Perhaps he has information."

"But Giles—" Andrew wavered.

Giles stared him down, calm and certain.

"Yes, Giles. If he wakes…"

Andrew wanted to stay with Max, but Giles would not be denied. "Very well. I'll be back soon." He slipped out the door after kissing Max on the forehead, his mind racing.

"Please don't be Lionel," he murmured to the club at large.

Lionel was his best friend, his mentor, and the first man he'd fallen in love with, even if they hadn't been a match. They had weathered many storms together.

He ran downstairs, ignoring how the walls tried to appear to be melting. He tried the billiard room first.

Nothing. Not a soul.

Oh, Giles. Something is wrong, friend. Very wrong.

He checked the public dining room. No one. The great room? Nothing.

Andrew turned and ran back upstairs, bypassing the second floor in favor of heading up toward the owners' suites.

The arm that shot out as he rounded the third floor landing took him utterly by surprise, clotheslining him and sending him wheeling. He staggered back, clutching his throat with one hand, groping for the newel post with the other so he didn't fall.

Lionel stepped out from the shadow. "Now, now, boy. Where do you think you're going?"

The familiar voice dripped with malice, with a somehow oily evil.

"Oh, Lionel." Something else was in there. Something that was not his friend. Andrew had seen this before once, at an army hospital. Whatever it was in Lionel, it had a vast, primal rage built up. Andrew scooted to one side, ready to slip around Lionel and call upon Matthias.

"No. No, I think you should stay. Your newest paramour is fascinating, don't you think? He just gathers things to him, like dust."

Andrew nodded slowly, watching Lionel like a hawk. "He collects. What do you want?"

"Guess." Lionel advanced upon him, eyes yellow, inhuman, so wrong, and when he licked his lips, the serpentine tongue was black as pitch, forked at the end.

"You can't have Max. You can't have Lionel, either." He would make a stand and soon enough others would join him. Hopefully the spirits would alert Max, if his lover would just wake.

"I already have this body. I will drain it and then I will have yours."

"No." Where was everyone? Goddamn it, he needed Matt or Julian. Or Giles.

"They can't see us. This place—I've been exploring all the spaces. It's quite apt at hiding things. Many things."

Shit. Of course. Elements of the club were always at odds with the people trying to contain it. There was a veil separating him from the other members. Andrew cast out with his mind, trying to see if anyone was using a talent to break through.

"I don't think so, dear boy. I've had you in so many ways. Consider what's to come the ultimate in submission."

He fought to scream, but a preternaturally strong hand wrapped around his throat, squeezing hard, driving the sound from his lips and the light from his eyes.

"ANDREW!" Max bolted out of the bed, trying to run to his lover, even as his legs were trapped by the bedsheets and he went down in a heap. "No! Andrew! Fuck!"

Max tore at the cloth, battering at the hands that tried to stop him. His lover was caught. Trapped. Hurt.

"Max! Max, stop it. You fell down the stairs."

He knew the voice, but he only placed it when he looked at Giles, who held his shoulders, keeping him down.

"Giles. Andrew. He has Andrew."

Giles would help. Giles must.

"Who has him?" Giles frowned now, and his body was surprisingly strong under that dapper tweed he wore.

"The demon! The demon wearing Mister Lionel's skin!" Weren't people listening to him? He knew what it was now, had awakened with Andrew's silent scream in his head.

Giles' brows rose to his hairline. "Lionel? Damnation, I sent Andrew to him."

"He's…" Whispers filled Max's head, images, as if all the spirits were talking to him at the same time. "He's hiding. Here. Right here, like a disease in the shadows."

Max levered himself up. "We have to find him. If you're there, my friends, my spirits, help me."

He had no idea if it would work, but he'd never done anything yet that he was sure of. He saw absolutely no reason to fret about that fact now. He needed his spirits to guide him now more than ever.

"Max, no." Giles pulled him to his feet, then helped him sit on the bed when his head spun. "You've been hurt. You must wait here. I will go and find Matthias."

"No. No, we don't have time. Come with me. Hurry." He stood again, refusing to release Giles' hand. "He's in here. How did he get in? We have to get him out."

"I— All sorts of things slip in here. We have wards, though. How did…" Giles stumbled, then straightened, following him. "I thought I had banished it when you fell. I had no idea it was in Lionel."

"Squatting like a toad."

And about to break free.

His Andrew was in danger. He towed Giles out into the hall. "Where? Where is he?" He would follow the lead of his spirits. They would be able to go where the not Lionel thing was.

He scrambled around in his pockets, desperate to find something, anyth… There. There. He pulled a coin from his trousers and held it out on his hand, palm up. "Show me. Please. Show me where he is."

The coin shook from side to side, then rose off his hand. Giles clapped, making a delighted sound, and Max glared at him.

"Sorry. Sorry. That's just so very interesting."

"I'll let you study me after we find Andrew and kill the demon, fair enough?"

"Enormously reasonable, yes."

"Excellent." He watched the coin, and it whipped past Giles, moving almost too fast for him to follow. Max ran, and when the coin disappeared through a wall, Max closed his eyes and lunged, expecting to smack his face, hoping instead that he made it through.

He popped through the wall, the sensation strange enough that it left him breathless, shocked. He glanced behind him, but Giles hadn't made it through. Max was on his own.

Max looked about. So, this was a replica of the club wherever it was. He knew the club better now than he had. What did Lionel like? Billiards?

Yes. Billiards. As the idea entered his mind, the room lit up, the tables appearing from smoke.

"Care to play, Maximillian?" Lionel's voice echoed around him oddly, and he didn't know the man well, but he knew this wasn't right.

"Of course." He knew the game far better now, thanks to Andrew, and he trusted that his good friends, his spirits, would support him. He needed time. "For what odds?"

"Hmmm. I think we might as well lay it all out on the table. If you win, you get your precious lover."

When he won. He refused to doubt. "Unharmed and well."

"Clever boy. Fine, but you must find your own way back."

"I will and he'll come with me."

"Ah, but the other terms... If I win, I keep either you or your Andrew. Your choice."

"Fine." Excellent. His lover was safe, no matter the outcome.

That suited him to the bone. "What about Lionel?"

"He's dying." The not Lionel flipped a languid hand. "Broken. You can't help him."

"Still, if I win, I want him too. He deserves that." Lionel loved Andrew. That was enough.

"Oh, how very noble. Especially since you let me in, pretty boy."

"I did not." But a part of him worried that he had, that somehow he'd allowed this evil in his home.

"You should begin." The demon smiled, his teeth black and sharp and awful.

He carefully chose his cue, lining up his first shot, using nothing but skill for this.

The ball rebounded once before coming to a complete halt in the middle of the table. "You're cheating, demon. This is a test of skill."

"Indeed. All of our skills." That awful smile came again, oil dripping from the lower lip.

"All of them?" *Help me. Please. For Andrew.* He willed the ball to move, to click two balls in a totally improbable pattern.

The ghosts answered him, the ball moving perfectly. The friction the demon put against it was obvious, but his spirits worked for him.

A long snarl buzzed through the air, but he refused to acknowledge it. He wouldn't share a bit of himself.

The demon gestured. "Still your shot, boy."

"I'm not your boy." He took another shot, then another, the spirits fighting the demon, again and again. He could feel himself fading, his wounds becoming harder and harder to ignore.

"Max?" His name was a tiny thread of sound. "No. Max, get out." Andrew. He couldn't see his lover, but that voice was unmistakable.

"I'm going to get you out, Andrew. No worries."

"Max...."

He didn't show it, he hoped, but hearing Andrew gave him

a surge of hope. Of energy. Of course, that meant he missed his next shot.

"My turn." Lionel's face was cracked, torn at the edges, blood leaking out.

"Be careful. That doesn't belong to you."

"Oh, but it does. And when I'm done with this husk, I will fuck your lover from the inside out. I will tear him apart."

"You will not. No matter whether you win or lose, Andrew is safe. You've given your bond."

"Now, sweet baby, I said it was your choice. I wouldn't make it until self-preservation kicks in. You might save yourself." The demon laughed, the sound like dry leaves in a graveyard.

And that was it, wasn't it? A demon didn't understand this basic fact. He loved Andrew more than he feared death.

The whispers came again, sweet and soft this time, approving. He wasn't certain he wanted to hear the spirits talk to him once this was over, but right now it was good to know he wasn't alone.

"Max. Max, go. Go while you can."

"Andrew, I love you dearly, but you really need to hush."

Andrew laughed, which seemed to enrage the demon. Maybe Lionel was still in there, and hearing Andrew made him stronger.

"Fight him, Lionel. Help me win."

The demon roared, but he missed the next shot, which meant Lionel had heard him. There was still hope there.

"Thank you. I appreciate the help." He made his play, tasting blood in his mouth, each breath seeming to creak. Tired. He was growing more and more tired.

The whole weight of the world was on him, dragging him down.

"Yes. You see now, don't you, boy? You can't beat me. I'll use them all against you."

"I've already beaten you, demon."

"No." The demon roared, and every ball on the table rose up and flew at him. Looked like someone was done playing.

Most of them stopped, but a few got through, catching him

in the shoulder, in the hip. He heard bones crack and his legs failed him. Still, the game was his.

Andrew was safe.

"Run, Andrew!"

Andrew rose, unsteady, from someplace that perhaps hadn't been there only moments before. "Max." The desperation in that beloved voice tore at him.

"Go! I'll bring Lionel."

Andrew wavered, distracting him for a crucial moment and he never saw the ball that cracked against his temple.

The last thing he saw was his lover.

Chapter Twelve

No!" Andrew lunged, catching Max as he fell to the floor. His body felt sluggish, as if it was not his own, but he fought with everything he had to stay conscious, to carry on the battle. He'd done that once before during the war. Dripping blood from a ball that had caught his arm, staggering through the fire and the screams.

This was worse.

"He's mine now." Lionel's beloved visage was unrecognizable, was twisted and sickening.

Andrew swallowed back bile at the thought of losing his beloved friend to this beast. "No. You forfeited the game. He wins." He tugged Max back toward the wall. He knew he'd come here through a wall.

"Only if he finds his way out before he dies," Lionel sing-songed.

"You're not Lionel." He had to remember that. Andrew pressed against the wall with his back, trying to find the tear in the dimension.

"No. I'm simply wearing his miserable body like a suit." The creature tore at Lionel's chest, leaving swaths of scratches.

Sheer horror threatened to turn him into a gibbering idiot, but he refused to allow it. He was a soldier. He would not lose Max and Lionel both. Andrew swallowed back his fear. "You're saying Lionel is too weak to be a challenge. So why didn't you take me? Or Max?" He had to buy time. For all of them.

"I wanted your boy. He feeds so many that I knew he could feed me, especially here."

Then it was good that Max was out cold. He wasn't such

a beacon when he slept. Andrew had to think of something, though, and soon.

"Lionel? Lionel? Please, is anything left of you in there?"

Lionel's face pulled back into its own shape for a bare moment, a horrific grimace of pain right there. "Kill me, Andrew. Please."

"I won't let him have you. You are my dearest friend, my confidant." *Fight him. You must fight him.*

Lionel's agony came through so clearly, but Andrew knew he was rallying, fighting the demon. That might earn them some time, and Andrew reached out with his talent, hoping someone was on the other side of the wall trying to get in.

He grabbed Max's hand, praying that the spirits clinging to his lover would respond, would call to Giles, to someone. Anyone.

The wall shook behind him as if someone was pounding on it, trying to break through. "Yes. Lionel! Call to them. Show them the way."

"NO!" the demon roared, the entire world seeming to shudder with the sound. The room's furnishings turned to dust, the scent of decay unavoidable.

Max squeezed his fingers. "Giles. Giles, in here."

"Damn you!" The demon charged at them, Lionel's hands spouting claws, curled into deadly fists.

The wall behind Andrew split, the fabric of the club breaking in two, the demon flying backward.

Giles seemed to glow in the darkness, but that was nothing— nothing to the blinding white light that Matthias and Koni brought with them, the lovers hand-in-hand like avenging angels.

Andrew slumped, his relief crushing, his hope a terrible thing. He pulled Max into his arms, shielding him.

The demon tore at Lionel's flesh and Matthias pulled a knife, pointed at the center of his old friend's chest. Koni began to speak—the sound of the guttural language seeming to drive into the demon like nails.

Max groaned, obviously fighting to stay awake. "Fight him,

Lionel. Force him out."

He loved Max more then than he ever had. Max was fighting for Andrew's friend just because he was Andrew's friend. He barely knew Lionel. Giles advanced as well, holding some sort of bottle and tiny silver clock. His Latin mixed with Koni's native language a strange harmony.

All the while Matt pointed the knife in the center of Lionel's chest, keeping him pinned. The demon couldn't move or his shelter would be destroyed. Lionel's very being shimmered, the demon undulating on a different plane.

"Help him, please," Max whispered, and Andrew wasn't sure whether Max was talking to him or the spirits that aided him.

Giles drew sigils in the air, Koni seemed to sway, almost dancing, but Matt stood solid and steadfast. Andrew wanted to do more, so he closed his eyes and sent whatever strength he could to his friends, hoping it would buffer them.

"Please. Please, it hurts." Lionel's cry broke his heart.

The demon roared moments later. "I will destroy you all!"

"Not if I destroy you first, demon." Matthias' voice was ice, slicing through the air.

"No." Max stood, stumbling forward and grabbing Lionel's hand and yanking hard, forcing Lionel away even as Matthias lunged forward, pinning the demon's true form to the wall. The demon screamed as the blessed blade sank deeper, Giles and Koni's voices almost a scream.

"Andrew. Andrew, take him out!" Max collapsed in a tangle with Lionel.

He would take them both out. Damn it all, that was the least he could do in this fucking mess. Never leave a fallen comrade behind. The demon's roar shook the whole world, he thought, and the smell of fire made Andrew duck his head and grab Lionel and Max, dragging them away from the chaos, the swirling wind becoming a tiny tornado where the demon was pinned by the sacred blade.

Let those more suited to that war battle it. He needed to get them out and get them help.

All of them.

Somehow, perhaps it was Max's spirits helping, he stumbled through back to Club Raven. A whole host of men were there, jumping into action when he pushed Lionel out, then dragged Max with him.

Dr. Benjamin Halliwell was there immediately, barking orders. "Get Lionel on the litter and take him to the room downstairs. Now! Alan, James, get Max and Andrew to their room. Andrew, Max is not to move until I can attend him. He must rest. Make sure he's not bleeding, and keep him quiet."

"I can do that. Lionel?"

"Do as I say!" The snap of command was enough to force everyone into action, including him. Ben must have been a hell of an officer.

Andrew had to make his choice, and he went with Max, David carrying his lover while Alan helped him limp upstairs. He would get news of Lionel as soon as he could.

They eased Max into his bed, and Alan touched his arm when he sank down on the mattress. "I'll send Daniel with hot water and towels. Bandages. David will be just outside keeping watch."

"The danger is being dealt with." Of that he had no doubt.

"Yeah." Alan's crooked grin made Andrew try to smile back. "Matthias and Koni and Giles? Unbeatable combination."

If they'd only come sooner. Before…

He reached out, stroking Max's pale cheek.

Alan slipped away, and Andrew climbed into the bed with him, covering them both to ward off shock. "Please let him wake up," Andrew whispered. "Please."

He had no idea who he was praying to, but he hoped someone was listening.

Well, anyone who wasn't a malevolent demon. They'd already played out that scenario, and honestly, he had learned everything that could teach him.

When Max woke, he had a moment of complete disorientation. He had no idea where he was, but he knew the last thing he remembered was fighting a demon.

He opened his eyes, the light too bright for a moment, so he closed them again.

"Beloved?" Andrew whispered. "Wake up for me."

"Andrew." The demon. The demon had Lionel and Andrew would be next. "You must run."

"No, love. No, the battle is won. I need to see you look at me. Please." Andrew stroked his cheek, which ached like he had a sore tooth.

"It's gone? You swear? You're well?"

"I am recovering." Andrew laughed, the sound wry, so Max opened his eyes.

"Oh, poor love." Max stared at Andrew, whose face and neck bore lurid bruises in many colors. He reached up, his ribs groaning, creaking. Still the feel of Andrew's skin was welcome.

"Shh. Benjamin says the more you lay quietly the faster your cracked bones will heal." Andrew closed his eyes now, pain chasing the smile away. Agony for him, Max thought.

"Lionel? Was I too late?" He had seen the pain the demon had wrought, and he prayed that Lionel was free.

"He lives." Andrew's eyes opened again, blue and clear and worried. "Benjamin says it's a matter of time now. He's deep inside himself, hiding, I think."

"His world was a horrific place." Who knew how long that demon had lived inside the man?

Andrew nodded solemnly. "I know. I wish he had told me how unhappy he was. That's the only way the demon could have gotten in."

"The demon said it was me. That I brought it in."

"No." Andrew was very firm. "No, love, it could have come from anywhere. This place does call to all manner of beasts. It wanted to feed from you. You are a feast, hmm?"

"I am? Am I a danger to the club?"

"Giles says no." Andrew sighed. "Though he wants to do

more training. Before we leave he wishes to speak to us."

"Leave?" Panic ripped at Max. He would do anything to protect Andrew's place here. "They're kicking us out?"

"No! No, we'll go home to finish convalescing, that's all."

Home.

Home.

The word echoed inside him, sweet and low.

Not to Andrew's house. To their home. Together.

"I would love that," Max murmured.

"As would I. I thought...I worried I had lost you."

He reached up, his hand shaking with weakness. Oh, that hurt, but he wanted to touch Andrew's face. "We're still here."

Hopefully his gifts were still with him as well. He was too exhausted to even attempt to contact the ghosts. He hoped he hadn't lost them all to his injuries...

"Shh. We are. All of us. Now we need to rest, come back to ourselves."

"I can't keep my eyes open," Max murmured.

"Hush then." Andrew stroked his hair back off his face. "Rest, love. I know you're on the mend now, so I can sleep as well."

"Stay with me?" He needed to know Andrew was close.

"All the while, Max. I promise." Andrew chuckled. "Benjamin tried to get me to sleep elsewhere so I didn't hurt you. I told him to fuck right off."

The laughter hurt, but it healed as well, soothing something deeper than his body.

Andrew kissed his lips lightly. "I'll be right here."

"Thank you." His eyelids were so heavy and Morpheus called to him. He yawned, his jaw popping, his body stiff with pain for a moment before all his muscles relaxed.

"Sleep. All will be well. You have my word."

And Andrew's word was enough.

"I would like to move home for a time," Andrew said quietly. Max slept deeply, a healing rest, but Giles and Benjamin had come to see them.

"Do you feel it's safe, Andrew?" Giles asked. "He's incredibly vulnerable right now."

"Perhaps, but there are more entities here than out in the world," Andrew pointed out.

"He has a point, Giles, and they will be able to rest quietly without so many people tromping about."

Giles glared at the good doctor. "You're not helping me."

"My job is to help the patient."

"Be good, Doctor, or I'll sic a demon on you."

"Nonsense." Benjamin snorted. "You have no desire to find a new doctor." Benjamin gestured to Andrew. "Let me look at your throat."

He lifted his chin carefully, the stretch aching, but not agony, not like it had been.

"Much better." Ben prodded gently. "Yes, I think if you promise to take it slow, I can release you both to go home."

"You swear to tell me should anything untoward occur?" Giles looked so worried, face pinched, brows gyrating hysterically.

"I vow it." Andrew reached out to touch Giles' hand. "You're welcome to visit, you know. Max is determined to take you out for luncheon."

"Oh? Oh, that would be welcome. Most welcome. I do like exploring and Max knows the best places, or so I've been assured."

"He knows the harbor well." Andrew grinned, then sobered. "May I see Lionel?"

Benjamin nodded. "He is deeply wounded, but awake."

"He is?" Oh. Hope swelled in Andrew's chest. "I want to see him."

"Shall I stay with Max?" Giles asked.

"Please." Andrew crawled off the bed, then bent to kiss Max's forehead, which had furrowed. "I'll return in moments, love. I need to see Lionel."

"Tell him we're not angry with him." The slurred words were still clear enough to understand.

"I will." His generous love. Andrew pulled on a dressing gown over his nightshirt, feeling odd when he pushed into slippers. How long had it been since he dressed?

"Come with me. I'll lead the way." Benjamin smiled at him, the unscarred half of his face preternaturally beautiful.

He left the room, leaning on Benjamin's arm before he was halfway down the hall. He was sweating and panting by the time they got down belowstairs. Lionel was in the safety room deep in the lower level.

"Does he really need to be in here?"

"He was dangerously close to death and the bosses say everything he could use to protect himself has been stripped away. They've called for...Morgan? Is that correct?"

Shock lanced through him at the mention of Morgan Garrison's name. He'd left the club years ago, and even Lionel had not heard from him since. He thought no one knew where he was…

"Matthias knew his direction?"

"Yes. He and Julian and Tony met about it."

"Goodness." That was...unheard of. A massive step.

"Yeah." Benjamin gave him a wry glance. "Be gentle with him. He's still very confused."

"He's my oldest and best friend, Ben." Andrew would be whatever Lionel needed him to for the moment.

"Of course. Forgive me. Sometimes I forget the complications of human affairs."

He shared another glance with Ben, who was an odd duck, and stopped at the door of the safety room. He took a deep breath before he knocked, calming his nerves.

The door clicked, swinging open to reveal Julian in his shirtsleeves and trousers, bare feet oddly incongruous with his image. "Ah, Andrew. I was just reading to Lionel. Do come in."

"I am about to head home for a bit. I wanted to see him before I left."

"Yes, of course." Julian stepped back, allowing him inside. "Do you mind if I step out a moment?"

"I'll wait for you to return before I leave," Andrew promised. Julian would no doubt like to freshen up. He waited for the door to click shut before making his way to Lionel's bedside.

Oh, God in heaven. Poor Lionel was ravaged, his already gray hair bearing white streaks, and his face and chest were bandaged where the demon had ripped his skin. Those green eyes were dull as dried grass.

"Hello, my dear friend. May I sit?"

"Please." Lionel's voice was rough as Samuel's. Andrew knew a tiny bit of what that kind of pain felt like now, and it made him hurt for his friends.

"Thank you. What were you reading?" He picked up the book Julian had left behind. Verne's *A Floating City.* "Ah. It is amazing, hearing Julian read, isn't it? So English."

"I suppose so. I wasn't listening."

Andrew looked directly at his friend. "What were you doing?"

"Hurting. Trying not to remember."

He nodded slowly. Andrew dreamed at night of Lionel's face sliding away, the demon showing underneath. From the inside it must have been beyond horrifying. "I'm so sorry, Lionel. Sorry I didn't see it."

"How could you? The demon was sly. He lied to all of you. I let him in. I must have."

"Oh, Lionel." He reached for Lionel's hand, which was oddly frail. "Max thinks it was him. Giles thinks his wards failed. I worry it was me, after the séance… Who knows how he got in?"

"What am I going to do, Andrew? I cannot hide here until the end of time."

"Matt has sent for Morgan." He thought Lionel deserved to know his old mentor was on the way. No one else would warn him.

"Morgan?" Lionel seemed to honestly focus on him now, green eyes wide. "No. Why on earth?"

"I suppose they think you're broken." That had been what Giles said, what Benjamin had intimated. If Morgan could put a spark back in those green eyes, though, Andrew thought it worth it.

"You should have killed me, Andrew. It would have been a blessing."

No. Everything in him rejected that. "You'll recover." He rubbed that skinny hand with his fingers. "I didn't know you were so unhappy, my friend. Again, I am so sorry."

"I am glad that you've found someone of your own, someone to care for." When Lionel said it, there was not even a hint of irony or jealousy.

Andrew nodded, his smile impossible to hide. "I love him very much. He's… he's meant for me."

"He tried to save me. You know that. He doesn't even know me and he tried to save me." Lionel's eyes were wide, wondering.

"I know." Max had thought he was a criminal, but he was Andrew's hero. "He told me to tell you no one is angry."

"No?"

"No. We're worried, we want you better, but no one is angry."

"I imagine you haven't seen Matthias."

"You know he doesn't get mad," Andrew teased.

"I thought he'd kill me."

If Max hadn't pulled Lionel away, Matt would have, without question. He was a lion protecting the sacred ground of the club, their Matthias, and he'd lost to a demon once.

"I'm glad he didn't. I'm taking Max home to recover fully, Lionel. I want you to promise me you'll send for me if you need me. For any reason. I want to help."

"Tell them I don't need Morgan?"

"I can try." He tried more than once to find out what had happened when Morgan left, but Lionel would never talk about it. The simple fact was, Matthias had called, Morgan was coming, and Lionel would be delivered into Morgan's hands.

Andrew picked up the book. "Should I read to you? Would you rather tell me what happened? Benjamin swears confession is good for the body as well as the soul."

"I remember going to meet the lad at the front door, the one you said was interested in me, then there was fire. Fire and chains, screaming — I couldn't get free. I could only see out sometimes."

"You don't remember feeling odd before that?" Had Zane been involved? Surely not, but he would pass it on to Julian.

"I've felt odd for months, Andrew, like a cloud was following me, shrouding me at times."

Yes. That made more sense. If the demon had been cohabiting his body, Lionel would have felt poorly. Perhaps his decision to pursue Zane had made the demon take action, needing to stamp out any chance that Lionel's mood would improve.

They would never know, but he liked to believe that.

"I will sit with you, friend, until Julian returns."

"I don't need a nursemaid." Lionel sounded waspish, but his smile belied the tone.

"That is a question, for sure, but I'll stay with you, regardless." Andrew set the book aside in favor of taking one of Lionel's hands in both of his. "Do you remember the time we had to roust the ghost out of the kitchen? The soup kept getting laced with saltpeter."

"I thought none of us would ever come to fullness again."

"I know! Thank God for Benjamin." If Benjamin had recovered from his deadly war injuries and Samuel had… well, mostly recovered, surely so would Lionel. He told story after story, knowing Lionel knew them, but wanting his friend to laugh.

By the time Julian returned, Lionel was sound asleep, holding onto his hand, a vague smile on his face.

Julian stopped inside the door, chuckling low. "I should have known you could ease his mind. Thank you, Andrew."

"I'd like to see him again before he goes. I assume Morgan will take a few days to get here."

"Yes. He's been traveling, so he's deep in the territories somewhere. He has a few days by horseback before he reaches a train."

"I'll come over in a few days, then." He eased his hand away, and Lionel turned on his side facing the wall.

"Heal, Andrew, and heal your lad up. We'll have you back hard at work in no time."

"I believe it. Giles has many ideas." He shook hands with Julian. "Thank you. You and Matt and Tony. For everything."

"Bah." Julian ushered him out. "Go home. Rest. We'll all be here when you return."

"I count upon that fact, my friend." He stood upon surprisingly shaky legs.

"I do, too." Julian opened the door for him. "Daniel will help you back to your Max."

"Thank you." It never ceased to amaze him, Daniel's strength, how corporeal he could be.

He was glad to have the arm to lean on, and by the time he got back to Max, he was sweating and trembling and worn out. Getting shot had been far easier, though Andrew knew how lucky he was. So many of his army friends had lost limbs. He thought moving back home might wait until tomorrow.

"I'll make arrangements, Master Andrew," Daniel told him. "You'll have help."

"Thank you, Daniel. I fear we will need it."

Daniel nodded shortly, leaving them, but there was a tray on the bedside table with glasses of water and lemonade and a plate of nibbles for him to temp Max with.

Andrew had a molasses cookie, munching slowly, letting his shaking stop. His dear Lionel.

"Will he recover, Andrew?" Max watched him from bruised eyes when he glanced up.

"I don't know, love. He's given up a bit, I think. The owners have summoned his old mentor, and if anyone can make him come back to us, it's Morgan." He hoped. "Sweet biscuit?"

"Morgan? Have I met him?" Max took the cookie, then handed it back.

"No. He left a long while ago." Andrew chose a tiny sandwich instead, passing it to Max.

"Ah." The soft bread of the sandwich must have pleased, because it wasn't refused. In fact, Max took another as soon as he finished the first. Then a tiny demitasse cup of soup and finally some mousse. Thank goodness.

"Will we go home soon, Andrew? I feel like I only had the promise of your amazing quarters."

"Daniel says he will arrange help for us and we can go tomorrow." He knew the safety and quiet of his home would help them both. The club had a hum of psychic energy right now as everyone scrambled to decide what had happened.

"Tomorrow and tomorrow and tomorrow." Max settled back in the pillows with a sigh.

"I'll send word to Kenneth. I would rather have a private conveyance."

"La-di-da." Was that a smile?

"Might as well enjoy being filthy rich." He winked at Max. "Can I join you, love? I feel worn to the bone."

"Please. Please, Andrew. I feared I may lose your touch. I crave it now."

"Do you?" He slipped under the sheets after he removed his slippers and dressing gown. He took Max's hand in his, holding tightly. "I thought he would kill you."

"I knew you were safe. That was what was most important." Max's hand shook, but he touched Andrew's chest.

"You're a treasure. My treasure." He wanted Max healed, wanted all those bones knitted, all those bruises gone. Max was only allowed to wear his marks.

"We're safe now, hmm? He's gone? The...beast, I mean."

"Not even ash left. Giles did a full banishment after Matt

killed it." Andrew would trust that with his life.

"The other club? The...shadow rooms? Are they gone too?"

"I'm not sure. I think the club exists in many..." What? Planes? Dimensions. Was there a word for it? "Levels."

"I'm glad they found us—Giles and the others."

"You found the way in. You and the spirits. I was so proud."

"I am too. I used all I have learned and they helped me. They helped me save you." Max smiled, really smiled, for the first time in days.

"They did."

Max was blinking hard, and Andrew's heartbeat finally slowed. He thought they could sleep now. They had a long day ahead of them tomorrow, moving to his house, getting settled. "Have I told you, Max, how I adore you?"

"Yes, Andrew. Almost as much as I care for you."

"Oh, good." That was the most important thing, after all. They were together, alive and safe, and in love.

He thought he could live with just about anything else.

Chapter Thirteen

Kenneth? I'm starving. Can I nip something from the kitchen without losing a finger to Cook?" Max was restless. Bored. And yes, hungry.

Andrew was still treating him if he was made of glass. His only outing since moving into their home was to see Lionel before he left. Morgan had been there, impatient to take Lionel away.

Gracious, Morgan was… formidable. Forbidding. Better Lionel than he.

"I can protect you," Kenneth drawled, the stuff exterior faded now that they had become friends. "Come along."

"My hero." He followed like a pup, wagging his tail at the promise of a treat.

Kenneth snuck into the kitchen like a soldier crossing enemy lines at night. Cook could be hostile when she did not wish to be disturbed. Her temperament never showed in her food. She made sublime treats.

The scents of bread and roast floated on the air and his mouth began to water. He knew better than to touch, and he trusted that Kenneth would know what food was available and what was sacrosanct.

"Shh." Kenneth held up a finger to his lips, then slipped around the big table in the middle of the room. "Rolls. Meat and cheese. Cakes. Some pickles for Master Andrew."

"Perfect. He loves those." Kenneth was a fine cohort. The best.

"Ahhh! I will cut your fingers off, you cur." Cook came out

of the pantry like an avenging angel, and Kenneth shoved the basket of treats at him.

"Run!"

"Save yourself!" He did flee, heading for their quarters at a dead run, cackling madly all the way.

He had a feeling Kenneth deliberately got caught.

The door opened as he pelted up to it, Andrew blinking at him as he rushed past. "Max? What are you doing?"

"Stealing a snack?"

"Ah." Andrew peered into the hall before slamming the door shut. "That's almost more scary than a demon."

"Almost? That woman is fierce. Pickle?"

"Oooh." Andrew's eyes flared bright blue, and he took the pickle, crunching through it. "What else did you get?"

He dug through the big basket with the hand towel laid in it, tons of little plates and bowls inside. "Rolls. Butter. Cakes. Biscuits, savory and sweet. Some cold meats and cheese. Some kind of jam."

The list went on and on.

"Oh, you found a treasure. We have a feast!"

He nodded. "I was starving."

"You have no idea how glad I am to hear that." Andrew smiled, blond hair falling over his forehead, his fingers ink stained where he'd been signing documents. He was adorable.

"Yes? Would you hear of the other things I'm starving for?" He'd been convalescing for months, had been traveling for training at the club with Giles for weeks and Andrew treated him like he was spun glass.

Andrew paused with a roll halfway to his mouth. "Mmm. Yes?"

He built himself a sandwich. "I ache for your touch, Andrew, for the games that you promised me. I only had a taste of the treats to be had."

Andrew smiled, the gentle expression one he'd come to know best in the last weeks. "I've been waiting. I haven't wanted to hurt you, love."

"I don't wish to be harmed, but a little hurt, a sting, it would be welcomed."

"Would it, now?" Something changed in those blue eyes, anticipation rising in them.

"It would. If you still desire me, of course? If you still wish to see my arse draped over your lap."

Andrew dropped his roll, reaching immediately for Max. "I want."

"Yes?" He went, his hunger for his lover larger than for any food.

Andrew yanked him close, the tiny roughness making his heart pound. "Yes." Andrew kissed him hard enough he saw stars. He could crow—the pressure was unafraid, and he pushed close, letting Andrew feel his growing need.

They kissed for long moments before Andrew pushed him away briefly to move the snacks off the bed. Then Andrew attacked Max's clothing, fingers working buttons and straps.

He didn't help, wanting Andrew to work for it, to want him. It worked. Andrew was eager enough to fumble, but Max stood nude in mere seconds, his cock standing proud and hard.

Andrew tugged his prick, measuring him, then moved to pull his short hairs. "I will deal with these later. That was a lesson only half taught."

His nipples went tight, his cock bobbing as if it agreed. They hadn't even gotten to play after Andrew shaved him.

"For now, though, it has been too long since I warmed your tight little bottom."

"It has." And he refused to be ashamed of needing it. He and Andrew had worked too hard to find a balance, to allow Max to understand that there was no wrong if they both wanted it.

Andrew sat back on the bed, drawing Max down across his lap. One hand stroked Max's skin, making him tingle all over, and he spread, exposing himself.

Rewarding him with a slow stroke to his balls, Andrew

hummed happily. "I do love how responsive you are."

"I need you, Andrew." Simple as that. He craved this act, but he needed it from this man.

"Oh, love." He felt the air move when Andrew drew back his hand. The first smack still managed to surprise him, making him jump when it landed. Andrew wasn't holding back.

By the third blow he was rocking, moaning softly as his cock began to leak. He rubbed it against Andrew's thigh, but his lover stilled him.

"No, sweet. You must stay still." Andrew began the spanking again, one slap on each cheek, alternating. The burn grew, embers becoming an inferno, and he panted from the heat.

He wiggled, stopping when Andrew stilled again. "No! Andrew."

"I told you, love. Still." Andrew waited, making sure Max didn't move.

The man was going to kill him.

He might return the favor. Or bite Andrew hard. Something. He could take his licks, but this not moving was too difficult…

"Now, love, now you can move." Andrew slapped his thighs, making them burn. "I was so angry, seeing his marks on you. So mad. I wanted to mark you instead, and waiting was so damned hard."

"I'll wear them, Andrew! Forever, I swear."

"I know! I want more. I want you with me always." Andrew worked almost down to the backs of his knees, then back, and Andrew's cock prodded him through the loose trousers Andrew still wore.

"For eternity. More, love. Please. I want you." He would promise his soul, but Andrew already owned that.

"Where?" Andrew chuckled, hot fingers tapping his hole, which seemed like the only thing not on fire in his backside area right now.

"Now!" He belatedly understood that was not the answer to the question Andrew had asked.

"Get the oil, love."

When his feet touched the floor, Max almost collapsed with shock, but he realized Andrew was stripping, trusting him to grab the sweet oil they had used on his last stay. He scrambled for it, digging it out of the press and uncorking it to slick his fingers and press them in his aching body. He would be ready for his lover.

Andrew moaned, cloth flying, his usually neat lover just tossing the clothes aside. Then Andrew was pulling him close again, one finger sliding into him alongside his. The stretch brought him up on tiptoe, his entire body rocking.

"That's it. Show me how you love my touch. Show me how tight you are." Andrew's words were like another kind of touch, pushing him higher.

He bent over the bed, the offer clear. He was ready — all his aches were Andrew's now.

"Oh." Andrew put both hands on his ass, spreading his cheeks. Then one hand left his skin, and he hoped that was Andrew oiling his cock. He trusted that was the case, and he waited, spread wide, head on his hands.

Andrew moved close again, the tip of his hot, hard cock rubbing over Max's hole. The heat was shocking, even as raw as his spanked flesh felt. Andrew pushed inside him, the tiny bit of resistance giving way easily. He rocked back to take more, eager for that scrape along the nerves deep inside him. He heard Andrew's gasp, the low, raw moan that followed his motion.

Max felt powerful when that moan sounded. He understood that now. His control here was equal to Andrew's. He ran the game as much as his lover did, and he squeezed Andrew's cock tight, milking it.

Andrew's response was a sharp, quick blow to his backside, the sting rocking him.

Max laughed for sheer joy, his body alive in ways it never had been before. "More, Andrew. Harder."

"Soon, Max. This first." More blows rained down on his

skin, completely out of time with Andrew's slow thrusts.

His thoughts cracked down the center and he found himself spinning, the world tightening down to the sound of Andrew's hand on his skin.

Max panted, wanting the next slap as much as he wanted the next thrust. Then the spanking stopped and Andrew grabbed his hips, slamming into him.

"Love!" He screamed the single word, unconcerned if the staff heard him. No one there would judge him.

Andrew groaned, a deep, harsh sound, and moved faster, harder, their skin coming together like another kind of spanking. He could feel every single hair on Andrew's body where it met his blistered skin.

The bedcovers rubbed at Max's cock, the friction delicious. Even better when Andrew reached beneath him to grab his dick and tug.

"Yes. By the heavens, yes." His eyes crossed and his balls drew up tight.

"Soon, love. Soon." Andrew's voice came out rough as gravel, the desire for him perfect and wonderful.

"Soon." His hands were fisted into the bedclothes, his sight empty, his entire focus on his cock, Andrew's.

"I need to come, love." Andrew laughed, a soft, rough chuckle. "Come with me."

"It would…" He cleared his throat. "It would be my pleasure."

Andrew chuckled again, the sound husky, and popped his ass, sending him tumbling, seed spraying from him. Second later Andrew filled him, as well, deep inside. The feeling was like coming home after a long journey.

Perfect heat covered his back and pressed him into the mattress. He let go of the sheets, smoothing them with both hands.

"Thank you, love. I knew you would ask when you were ready." Andrew kissed the back of his neck.

"I should have asked a fortnight ago."

"Then I would have refused. You had to be healed."

Max rolled his eyes, but he had to smile. "Stubborn."

"I am." Andrew pushed him up on the bed and joined him, wrapping strong arms around him. "Especially where you are concerned."

"Indeed?" He found that idea most pleasurable.

"Yes." Andrew smoothed a hand down over his hip. "I think we should invite Giles out to lunch."

"I think that would be a lovely idea."

"Good. He's pushing for us to get back to work and wants to evaluate your progress."

Giles had sent him schoolwork of sorts. He'd been honing his skills for several weeks.

"I'll send a note." He lifted his face for a kiss. "Tomorrow."

Andrew gave it happily, kissing him until he could barely see. "We have much to catch up on today."

"Mmm." They did. Games. Kisses. Another bite or two of their stolen feast.

So many plans. Max grinned at the ceiling, ready to get back to his new life.

"So, where are we going? Are we going to an oyster house? Are we taking the horse car? I've been reading about how they think they'll replace the horse car soon with steam? Steam engines don't get the influenza."

Giles chattered non-stop as they left his house, almost bouncing with excitement. A carriage from the club had delivered him nearly half an hour ago, and he'd been putting Max through his paces ever since.

Clearly Giles had now decided it was time for lunch.

"No oyster house," Max said. "You indicated you wanted to rub elbows with a more common man."

"Indeed. You bring me fine men by the dozens. I want to meet everyone else!"

Andrew smiled as Max looked at him, murmuring, "We should take him to a bordello."

"We should. Today, though, I think we should take him to Marshall's Dining Rooms."

Max's face lit up. "Capital idea."

Marshall's was on the basin, serving five and ten cent entrees, including breakfast and dinner all day. Oatmeal. Cracked wheat with milk. Liver and onions. They served over 1500 meals a day to working men and women. Giles would expire from sheer joy.

"Show me," Giles demanded. "Show me everything. Will we see Remy as well? Shall we invite him?"

"Mmm. I doubt Remy will join us. Isaiah and Jean might be willing, if I send them a note?" Andrew asked both Max and Giles, not wanting to overstep and ruin the experience.

"Oh, yes. I love to share new experiences with friends!"

"Max?"

"I think that's a fine idea. If you send a runner, they might arrive at the same time we do."

"Kenneth! I need to send a message to a friend!" Andrew laughed, getting into the spirit of the adventure.

"Of course sir. I'll call one of the runners up." He had to admit Kenneth was almost pleasant these days. The man liked Max; they were in cahoots against Cook, who seemed to be having the time of her life these days. She'd made some sort of Austrian torte the other day just because she wanted to try the recipe. Andrew thought he'd gained five pounds.

"Off to the horse car. Did you bring dimes, Giles?"

The bespeckled man held up a purse filled to the brim with coin and Max blinked. "Lord. You'll get beaten down for that."

"Should I leave some here?" Giles looked a bit uncertain. "No one needs another beating."

"We'll definitely leave some here." Max glanced around before grabbing a china bowl from a nearby table. He poured more than half of the coin out. "There you have enough to try one of everything on the menu and still take the horse car anywhere you want to go."

"Really? Marvelous!' Giles tucked the purse away in his pocket.

Max shot Andrew a look as he shifted from foot to foot. Someone was feeling him today—both the flogging and the shaving. Wonderful.

Definitely delicious. Moving about would be torture all day, and Andrew would offer relief once they returned home.

"Shall we go, beloved?" Max asked, eyes twinkling with pure merriment.

"Yes!" Giles took them both by the arm and dragged them out into the street. The man was a menace, but by the time they reached the nickel lunchroom, Giles had invited two dock workers and a horse cart driver to their luncheon, their new friends chatty as hell.

He wasn't sure when his life had become like this, how his father's son was traveling to eat at a lunchroom with a sorcerer, a pirate, a thief and his lover.

Whatever it was that had happened, Andrew was grateful as hell. He had Max, had what he had always wanted. A partner in… well, not crime, certainly, but life.

He glanced at Max, watching him laugh at something Giles had said.

Max was no charlatan, and Andrew never had to be worried about debunking him. No, he had a feeling from now on Max would be a happy medium.